This book is the epitome of cool. A cross between *Twenty Four Hour Party People* and Tom Perrotta's *The Leftovers*, written by Julian Barnes. It contains a narrative as spiky as a punk set, a whole symphony of ideas composed by Mankowski within a few subtle bars of text. A brilliantly written literary treat.
AJ Kirby, reviewer for *The New York Journal of Books*

Anyone who remembers *Melody Maker*, or who attended indie nights in clubs strewn with snakebite, will fall in love with this book immediately. Mankowski captures brilliantly the psychology of 'fan obsession'. Those of us who marvelled at 'The Secret History' or 'A Passage To India' are sure to find it enthralling.
Matthew Phillips, *Huffington Post*

Already recognised as a major rising talent, Mankowski here establishes himself as a significant voice in British fiction with a novel that will raise knowing smiles from the rock cognoscenti, plaudits from literary critics, and will captivate readers every-where. This is clearly a writer of great talent.
Andrew Crumey, author of *Pfitz and Sputnik Caledonia*, longlisted for The Man Booker Prize

Mankowski creates a very convincing band and history. The novel has a lot of classic story lines – the search for the missing hero, the last chance at dreams and ideals, the tension between a 'real' job and an artistic life – along with a thriller element. It's funny too, at times I laughed out loud. With the character of Robert Wardner I felt he was channeling The Manic Street Preachers' Richey Edwards, The Fall's Mark E Smith and Joy

Division's Ian Curtis simultaneously. Very powerful. There's so much about this book that people would enjoy. I really enjoyed it. **Lyn Lockwood**, Chief Examiner for A Level Creative Writing, AQA

Guy Mankowski's latest novel, *How I Left The National Grid*, showcases the rich research, scintillating prose, and psychological depth that characterised his earlier books. Here, though, those qualities are used to bring to life a potent and still vital place and time in British culture: post-punk Manchester. Set in the present, but reflecting on the past, *How I Left The National Grid* reveals that so much of where we are now grew from who we were then. Flashbacks and corrupt memories flesh out the ambitions of a band formed in those past moments, in vivid, haunting, and haunted scenes. But readers can also experience the thrill of the chase to find people who do not want to be found in the present. In doing so, we are forced to ask: what becomes of our dreams? Mankowski's original and captivating alternative history depicts the conflicted start of a turbulent era when we were told there was 'no alternative', and thereby perhaps sketches a different landscape for the future.

Dr. Adam Hansen, editor of *Litpop: Writing and Popular Music* and author of *Shakespeare and Popular Music*

How I Left The National Grid

A post-punk novel

How I Left
The National Grid

A post-punk novel

Guy Mankowski

Winchester, UK
Washington, USA

First published by Roundfire Books, 2015
Roundfire Books is an imprint of John Hunt Publishing Ltd., Laurel House, Station Approach,
Alresford, Hants, SO24 9JH, UK
office1@jhpbooks.net
www.johnhuntpublishing.com
www.roundfire-books.com

For distributor details and how to order please visit the 'Ordering' section on our website.

ISBN: 978 1 78279 896 5
Library of Congress Control Number: 2014954852

A CIP catalogue record for this book is available from the British Library.

Design: Lee Nash

Printed and bound by CPI Group (UK) Ltd, Croydon, CR0 4YY

We operate a distinctive and ethical publishing philosophy in all
areas of our business, from our global network of authors to
production and worldwide distribution.

ROBERT WARDNER

It's hard to remember what it was like being onstage on Top Of The Pops. *However bright and emotional and vivid it was, it becomes kind of inert. I can remember certain neurons being fired in my brain though. Pleasure impulses I'd not experienced before, or since.*

In 1981 we were properly famous. Schoolchildren saw me as 'that alien bloke off Top Of The Pops.' *My mother got hassle off chippy journalists coming into her salon and asking if it were true that I'd been sent from the future. And she would say no, it wasn't, because she distinctly remembered giving birth to me in a bathtub in Hulme, in 1955.*

It just happened suddenly. It was weird, because overnight all the ideas I'd scrawled in my notebook, which would have got thrown away if I'd left them on the bus, were suddenly a source of massive speculation. It was as if by being on the front of magazines and on TV I'd cracked something and now I had all the answers. No wonder it seemed as if we were from the future. Our single, 'The Commuter Belt', was released with the record company hoping for no more than it might chart. It went to number 4. Daydreams about what I would do if I got on TV had to become a reality in a matter of days.

First thing, we got some money off the label and went to a military surplus store in Manchester's Piccadilly Gardens. I wanted us dressed in urban camouflage when we went on TV, like we'd been fighting guerrilla warfare. But they only had four of these black security guard outfits so we had to make do with them. They had badges on, saying 'I'm...and I'm here to serve.' I ripped them off, so we definitely wouldn't look like traffic wardens.

Regardless, I was going to make an impact. Millions of people would be watching, and I was about to do something that would scorch my face on their retinas. I didn't know what, but I knew I wasn't going to miss the opportunity.

Bonny put the four of us on a bus to BBC Studios. Jack nervously drummed against my seat the whole way there, Theo kept saying, 'We've got to do something outrageous. Television is the only way to teach people how to behave these days.' I just drank my whisky and told him to stop twisting about. Simon knew I was working on a plan.

I'd been preparing for this for almost ten years.

That was the first time I went onstage as Clive Douglas, not as Robert Wardner. For years I'd been thinking about Clive. Some worker drone trapped in a power plant, on a shift that refused to end. Thinking about what he would do if he ever got the chance to show the world how he felt. That night, I'd perform as him. Twitchy, black-eyed, desperate. Starved of sunlight, bewildered by technology. Flailing about, spiralling into panic. Just behind me onstage, like a watchful supervisor, Simon would be playing guitar.

All the other bands were asking the girls in the makeup department to make them look tanned, though I doubted they'd ever been anywhere hotter than the Isle Of Wight. Singers in those days usually requested the wardrobe girls find them sweaters to put over their shoulders, so it looked like they'd just come off a yacht. They weren't used to being asked to make them as white as possible, like I did.

I wanted us to look like we were no longer human. I wanted to make the point that the most alien amongst is the most familiar. That a human being, gradually messed up by night shifts and low pay, could eventually look as if they'd fallen from Mars.

The makeup girl used thick, sharp lines of dark paint under our eyes to make them more pronounced. Theo was the only one who broke our uniform code. He wore his younger sisters' undersized black leather jacket, complete with this ridiculous fur trimming. We couldn't have predicted that soon everyone would be wearing an exact copy of it.

The studio was dowdier than I'd ever imagined. Small and badly-lit, but still that feeling in my stomach wouldn't settle. As the moment for us to go onstage neared everything sped up. Some bloke with elbow patches, who looked like he'd just come off University Challenge, came into the dressing room and told us to listen closely for onstage instructions. Play the game, he said, you're lucky to be here. I asked him when we would get to check the sound levels, and he stared down his crooked nose and said, 'I wouldn't worry about that, son, no one is going to be listening to you.' The rest of the band looked at the floor but I slowly clenched my fists.

'I'll make sure they catch every second,' I thought.

We were given various orders, all of which we solemnly accepted and straight away ignored. I wasn't going to get pushed about by Henry Kelly. He abandoned us the minute The Human League came flouncing round the corner. Their singer, with his long black hair pulled back over a diamond earring, looked Theo up and down and shuddered. Then all these young girls started screaming when a Latino woman in a red flamenco dress came round the corner with a clipboard, showing Julio Iglesias the way to the stage. Simon looked at his healthy face and deep leather tan, then looked and me and said 'I think you'd better start taking some vitamins, Rob.'

As Iglesias' entourage came past us they pushed Simon out of the way, his guitar dropped to the floor and a string broke, seconds before we were due to go on. Iglesias didn't even apologise. He was a love-god, and we were dirty guttersnipes from Manchester. That was the picture. I thought, right, that's it.

Bonny told us to focus. There was steel in her eyes, then, hard as the cut of her bob. I think she saw in us a way to make her mark on the world. Prove to herself she could be a figure other women looked up to. Sometimes we needed her ferocity. I remember them lining us up in the wings before we went onstage and the look on her face was just unforgettable. Even she thought this wouldn't happen so soon. 'Don't blow it, Rob,' she kept saying. 'Remember what we've all given to get you to this point.'

We were cooped up in the corridor, and through a crack in the door I could see aimless young girls going into the studio, all oversized sweaters and white dinner jackets. Jimmy Savile was giving them party hats and streamers to chuck about, getting some of them to drape them over him. He was like this manic jester in the middle of it, a bit unhinged. There was this feeling building in the air, this tightening of the moments that I'd never known before. Every inch of clothing you had on, every expression you gave was being carefully scrutinized. As the room filled with young bodies, clutching their chests and looking around them, I realized that with one gesture I could cause an explosion. With one statement, one movement, one act, I could sweep away all the polystyrene and lights and make everyone at home sit forward. But I still didn't know what I'd do.

The pressure to conform was incredible. You felt yourself doubting everything about you, especially when elbow patches told us we wouldn't get to practice being onstage, because Iglesias had taken our spot. I rallied the four of us together in that little corridor, skinny limbs in black against this sea of white casual day-wear. I told the boys nothing was going to shake us off course, this was our chance. We were going to blow the roof off the place and we were going to do it our way. Forget all the party poppers and bunting, I said. Let's introduce something real here. Show the world what a charade this all is.

Simon was shaking as the girl pointed us to the stage. The stage was a small black square, set amongst a background of grey plastic cubes and dry ice. The lights were down, in seconds they were going to go up.

When we went through those doors we looked like we'd crawled out of the underworld.

We were pushed onstage, into a bath of boiling light. Jack squirmed onto his drumming stool, Theo squinted out at the waiting crowd. Simon looked as if he'd forgotten how to hold a guitar, but seconds later he was grasping its neck as if his life depended on it. Already, the makeup was starting to run down our faces. I stood on the edge of the stage, looked out at the sea of silhouettes and tensed.

A second later Savile stepped into the crowd and introduced us. He made some joke about us being the runts of the litter and then I heard our keyboards blast through the speakers, thinner than usual, but growing louder. The lights went onto us. I grabbed the microphone.

I could just about make out all these young girls with hands on their hips. I had never seen them at our gigs before and yet the moment the track started they were screaming. It was almost as if their whole lives had been lived in preparation for seeing us play. I knew they would soon stop screaming when they heard our song.

I'll never forget that sense of seizing the moment. You have to make it out of absolutely nothing. It felt reckless and dangerous and there was genuinely no sense of what it might lead to.

Jack's drum-beat instantly connected with the crowd, made them move. Then that rich synth line filled the air and the audience cheered. Simon, visibly shaking, began miming energetically on his guitar. I felt my body crackle and twitch and I opened my mouth. I knew I would be singing over my own voice, but I wanted to do it with heart, and for people to see that. There was one sensational moment, like the moment a woman gives you as you pin her to the bed, when the whole audience looked up to me.

I tore into the song. I had laboured over every line, every last vowel and consonant, and I wanted to mainline it straight into every living room in the country. When it came to the bridge, where the band suddenly sped up, something took over my arms and I felt possessed by the need to make the band create a sound so huge and overpowering that the audience were permanently altered. The sheer force of the first chorus overwhelmed me, my voice urging its way through this thick storm to enhance the recorded vocals, stick onto the contours of every note and bury that damned hook in the mind of every terrified kid dreading school the next day, every dead-eyed office drone working for managers they loathed, every housewife longing for the visions of the future sent to her in adverts through the letter-box daily. Now is the time for revolution, I thought. I'll be the spark.

As the song reached its climax I tried to move to the front of the stage, and the whole of the front row moved forward to touch me. In the last verse, as I sang the refrain 'wind the commuter belt around your neck,' I lifted the microphone lead up to my throat. I decided in a split second what my one act of defiance would be.

I could see elbow patches watching from the wings. He met my eye as I stopped singing, and slowly shook his head. I could see all the smiles on the faces of the young girls as they sang along to this weird hit on *Top Of The Pops*. I could feel the sheer fear this one movement was provoking in the studio. Was he going to try choke himself with the mike lead on air? Elbow patches held a finger to his throat. The audience looked up at me, transfixed by my sudden lack of movement, my voice still audible even though my mouth was shut. As Simon sliced into the outro I threw the cord around my neck and pulled, hard. The air was forced out of my throat and I choked into the mike, which dropped to the floor with a loud bang. The audience gave off a huge, icy gasp. I fell onto my knees, putting my foot onto the lead to get some leverage, and then I yanked it hard. I don't know what came over me, but at that moment I sincerely wanted to do it. Choke myself to death, on live television. My eyes bulged, and I saw my knuckles turn white.

Elbow patches stormed over to Bonny, who was already smiling. He gestured at the stage, and she shrugged, a smile on her face. He pointed at the sound desk, and a moment later, the backing track stopped.

The audience were no longer dancing. The sound faded, as I writhed on stage, winding the cord round and round my neck, my free hand clawing for air. I looked up, and my vision started to narrow. Every single girl in the audience was looking at me, confused, and I was slowly blacking out. But the one set of eyes I met, over by a pillar, were Bonny's. She looked back at me and nodded, calmly, as she folded her arms.

It took two security guards to pull me from the stage. As they unravelled the cord, the crowd drew back like closing blinds. Elbow patches ran up to me. 'You will never, ever play on this show again,' he said, spittle flying onto my face.

I got up, and shook my head. In the distance I could hear muted cheers. I gulped, and as she came closer Bonny held her arms out.

She and I both knew it would be all over the press the next day, that every playground and office would be buzzing with what I'd done. Every housewife would be terrified that their kids would buy our record.

That was exactly what happened.

1

'I think you deserve this treat,' Sam said, stepping ahead of Elsa and dramatically opening the door to the restaurant.

'Hmm,' she said, her eyes narrowing.

Sam watched the sunlight race over the windows, reflecting the silvery hue of the river beside them. He was still trying to find his way through this new world of bright, polished surfaces. He felt that for years he had lived amongst damp corners, in the dank atmosphere of bedsits. But taking in the sparkling cutlery, and the elegant dresses around him, he felt like he was finally stepping into the light. A blistering modern light, that blasted away the squalor of his past.

He looked at Elsa, who was taking in the hubbub. He considered her elfin, Gallic look, which still attracted so much male attention. Her floral summer dress displayed flashes of her legs that were a little too slim.

A waiter swept them to their upstairs table with a hearty wave. He seated them at a table close to the window, which overlooked a quayside blooming with sun. The river played upon the windows of the surrounding offices like a distant mirage.

Elsa loved these displays of chivalry from Sam. In the early days he would take her for dinner even when he evidently couldn't afford it. Once or twice an extra drink had been too much, and he'd had to offer to wash up, but he'd been useless even at that. But this time she suspected there was more to it than just generosity. He kept pulling the slightly dirty curtains of his Mowgli-style hair out of his large, blue eyes.

'I wish I wasn't going to dinner with all this dust in my hair,' she said, coiling a blonde lock around her finger.

'We've been working all day,' Sam said, his eyes scanning over the menu. 'Everything's in the house now. Besides, this is my treat. I want to talk to you.'

She ordered a glass of white wine and concentrated on Sam. 'You want to talk to me?' she asked. 'What does that mean?' She paused. 'It's about that phone call, isn't it?'

He took her hand, and she offered in return a small smile. 'I'm so glad that we've taken the plunge and got a place together,' he said.

She laughed. 'Give over, Sam. I had to drag you kicking and screaming into any sort of a domestic life, and you know it. You'd have spent the rest of your life eating Super Noodles and wearing a sock for a belt.'

'I know. You were right,' he pressed. 'I couldn't keep living like that. I know it wasn't good for us.'

'Wasn't good for us? I think it would have been the end of us, Sam.'

The remark seemed to cause a pronounced drop in the temperature.

'Not quite,' Sam responded. 'I know this is my last chance. I'll become a proper man about the house. Changing light bulbs, using a feather duster.'

'You'd end up using it in the bloody toilet, Sam. Anyway, you don't have to worry about all that. We get a cleaner and have a caretaker. Part of the deal.'

'Does he know how to use the taps? Because I can't bloody work them out.'

'But I think that's part of the fun, you know?'

'Not being able to wash? Yeah, definitely.'

She tossed her head back. 'Don't be a twat. So who was this call from? A credit card company?'

He leaned in. 'No.'

'How could anyone else have got our number yet?'

'It was from a guy called Martin Graham. From this book publisher. Mason House.'

'Go on.'

'He's heard that Robert Wardner has been confirmed as alive, for the first time in twenty five years.'

'Oh god. That National Grid guy? Didn't he murder some girl?'

'That was never proven.'

'It was you who told me about it. Why else would he suddenly take off, vanish like that?'

'He was unable to finish this incredible record he was making. Now there's talk that he's going to reform the band and complete it. And this publisher was asking what I knew about it all.'

'Why?'

'Well, I'm guessing he wants someone to track down Wardner. Tell the story about how he vanished, in a book.'

She cocked her head. 'If he did kill someone, he's hardly going to want his story told, is he? If he's in the habit of killing people who intrude on his life, you're just going to make yourself a target.'

'I doubt it. I wrote some of the first major articles about him, ones that helped him get famous.'

'You were a teenager then. You can't be chasing after men like that in your forties!'

'But you don't choose when these opportunities come along, Elsa. This is my chance to finally make my mark on the world. Plus, I think it could make us some money.'

She pulled a bread-stick out of the basket, and looked as though she might snap it.

'The call centre work is regular though, Sam. Something we can rely on.' She closed her eyes for a moment. 'The house deposit cleaned us out. I can't see any way we're even going to make the first mortgage payment.' She folded her napkin into a tight, hard wad. 'Perhaps dinner wasn't such a good idea…'

'Elsa, if I can convince this publisher to give me a commission to write the book, it will more than pay for that first instalment.

Shifts at the call-centre certainly won't.'

'You'll be happier there once the regular pay starts to come in.'

'Elsa, it's bloody awful there, like being a hen in a coup. I want to do something creative with my life. How am I doing that now? I play on people's fears about getting burgled, to convince them to get stupid burglar alarms. When I can't even work the ones in my own house!'

'They're state of the art, that's why.'

'They're unnecessary.'

'And a book about Robert Wardner is necessary? Sam, come on. Not only is he dangerous but you…you could end up getting sick again. I couldn't bear it.'

'How would I get sick? I'd be getting that fire back in my life!'

'But that fire didn't do you any favours, did it? When you should have been at university like every other eighteen-year-old you were instead obsessing over them at home. By your own admission, that was the first step that ended with you getting…' She stopped herself.

'You can say it, Elsa. They won't ban us from coming here for olives if you say it.'

'Getting institutionalized.'

'But that wasn't just about them. And besides, I did go back to university, because otherwise we wouldn't be together, would we?'

'You went back eight years after everyone else.'

'That was because my head wasn't right, not because of the band. I had to do something with that time, which is why I used it to research them.'

'Perhaps a bit much? Come on, Sam, that counsellor said you needed to stay clear of anything dark. Especially now. We've worked so hard to get here.'

'All that will pay off now.'

'Well it doesn't seem a pay-off to me, Sam. Not on the day we had promised to leave all that behind. Come on, this is your last chance.'

'But you know it makes sense. Come on, Rodders. This time next year we could be millionaires.'

She smiled, and cupped her hand over his. The small silver ring on her middle finger sparkled for a moment in the white light. 'I love that you have this passion. I know it isn't easy for you right now, but this will pass.'

'Give me the chance to prove that it is possible, Elsa. That we don't have to spend our time on this planet doing things we detest.'

'Come on, it's not that black and white. Look at what's happened with me at the gallery. Any day now Malcolm is going to give me my first exhibition to oversee. Then we can start to have the sort of lifestyle a couple of losers like us could normally never get.'

'I'm not sure you working for Malcolm is picking up where Harold Pinter left off.'

A waiter drifted to her side. Elsa ordered a bottle of Cabernet Sauvignon, Sam consenting with a nod. As the waiter turned Elsa bowed her head again.

'It gives us the occasional holiday, Sam. Would it kill us to have one or two soft furnishings? But you'd have to give all that up to go off chasing after a murderer.'

'He wasn't a murderer! I'm not venturing into Colombia to discover the story of Pablo Escobar. Wardner was based in Manchester, and the recent sighting of him was in London. The biggest risk will be that I get short-changed for a baguette in Stepney Green.'

Elsa looked out at the river again. Sam knew she had always felt comforted by the thin belt of sparkling water running through the city, and the opulent houses built around it. She once said that they had seemed like a secret symbol, communicated from the city to her, telling her that this was the place she should build her future.

'I know that it could work,' she said. 'But I think it's far more likely that I'll end up funding this folly by putting in extra shifts. How on earth are we going to make the first payment as it is?'

'I think I could get an initial advance off him. This Martin sounded fascinated by the idea of a book. You know what these London types are like, always wanting to think they're one step ahead of the game. I'll just use that to get us a fat pay cheque.'

'You're not the entrepreneurial type, Sam. It wasn't so long ago you replaced a broken car window with a bin liner.'

'I can be entrepreneurial. I'll show you, Elsa. It will be my name on the front of the book. I'll get a suit. We'll have the book launch at the gallery...'

She laughed. 'And you and Wardner can dance the night away, looking deep into one another's eyes.'

He laughed. 'No, I'd dance the night away with you. He couldn't dance, anyway. Famously.'

'You're such a nerd.'

'This is the perfect time for this opportunity to have come. I have the space to write too now, I could use the spare room.'

'I was hoping we could keep the spare room free from books.'

'For what?'

'For a baby, Sam. I'm thirty five and we need to start building a nest.'

Sam hesitated. 'You really think I could be a father?'

She smiled. 'You were the one just trying to convince me you're the next Alan Sugar. Surely fatherhood will be a doddle after you've built your empire?'

The waiter appeared, pouring a flame of red wine into her glass. Sam saw how the sun lit the edges of Elsa's hair.

'So how about it? My last shot at fame and glory? Solving a great mystery before becoming the committed family man. What do you say?'

She smiled.

'Yes?' He leant closer. 'Elsa?'

She threw up her hands. 'You're going to do it anyway. What

different does it make what I say?'

'I am going to make you proud. I'll head down first thing tomorrow to get started. Now are we ordering, or what?'

Elsa looked down at the menu. Sam caught a glimpse of the whiteness of her knuckles, as slowly she began to clench her hand.

'Come on, have whatever you want, Elsa.'

Sam didn't recognise Elsa's expression.

'You're not really worried, are you?' he asked.

She looked up. 'Of course I am. It's not worth the risk. Sooner or later you're going to see that going after him is walking into your own damn grave.'

ROBERT WARDNER

People say that after Top Of The Pops *it's never the same, don't they? Well, they're right. Bonny called it 'our first assault on mass consciousness.' You can push for years, playing for a promoter who doesn't even turn up, in bars where they think you're a bunch of hairdressers just because you've got a keyboard. But once you've grabbed the world by the collar it keeps looking up at you, with morbid interest.*

After our performance we had so much energy. Theo was running up and down the BBC corridors. I asked him, 'What are you doing?'

He said 'I'm looking for Legs And Co.'

'What will they want with you?'

'I'm dangerous now.'

'What, for using curling tongs in the bath? Sit down.'

Me and Simon went for a swig at the fire exit. Trying to come down in the freezing wind. Still in our onstage gear, security guards in eyeliner. Knocking back a flask of cheap vodka.

'You're not going to believe this,' Simon said, trying to light a damp fag.

'What?'

'Julio Iglesias is only hanging around drinking bottled water in the corridor.'

'Who's that?'

'That lounge-lizard who knocked me guitar out of tune before we went on. No word of an apology.'

'That bloke singing in Spanish?' I zipped up my jacket.

His eyes got wider. 'No, Rob. Don't.'

I flexed my fingers.

'What you going to do?'

'I'll think of something. The Volvo's out the back. Maybe we can kidnap him for ransom? Get the Latin market to pay us some attention.'

I was down the hall before he could stop me.

Iglesias was there. Wavy hair, white-capped teeth, and water that had probably been cooled on the thighs of a virgin moments earlier.

'Julio, do you recognize us?'

It's quite a talent to be scared by someone and completely ignore them at the same time.

Simon wasn't far behind me. 'Yeah, Rob. He'll be a massive fan of our single about the Manchester commute,' he said.

At the end of the hall I could hear Bonny shout 'Rob. You've got to be shitting me. Leave him alone.'

'Do you recognise us Julio?' I asked.

He flashed a smile, just for a second. Took in the nail varnish and eyeliner and then with one pristine loafer took a small step back.

'Julio Iglesias, I'm arresting you for crimes against Latin culture. You do not have to say anything...'

Iglesias dropped his water. It landed on the floor with a muffled thump and started pouring out of the nozzle.

'Are you security guys?' he said. Eyes wide.

Bonny appeared out of nowhere. An ambassador's wife crossed with a stick-woman.

She pointed at her head, twirled a finger. 'They're from Manchester,' she said. 'They can't arrest anyone.'

Our next gig was a sell-out. When we pulled up in the decommissioned coach Bonny had got for us, this chorus-line of girls were waiting. Clutching thermos flasks and green pens.

Watching.

Theo thought that made us The Beatles. 'We're as big as The Beatles,' he'd say. 'Being this famous is scary.'

'We're nowhere near as big as them,' I said.

'You sure you want to be?' Jack asked. Look what happened to Lennon.'

Theo looked at the girls out of the window and said 'How are we not famous? All revolutions start with the hearts of teenagers.'

'Jesus. Shut up, Theo,' Simon said.

'I could sleep with any one of them,' Theo said. 'It's blowjob city out there.'

I took in the cardigans, pigeon-toed feet and spiral-bound notebooks. 'Where?' I asked.

I looked out at the crowd. It was like someone had gone around every disco, every remote railway station, every motorway café, and scooped up all the lost souls. Then put them all outside Newcastle City Hall. For us.

Every aspect of my life had become chaos since we'd been on TV. For months we'd had plans to have shots of city life blasted onto us while we played onstage, but could never afford it before. Whenever we tried the screen fell on Jack the minute he started drumming. Suddenly we could do whatever we wanted. Every waking hour all I could see was roadies, technicians, promoters. Coming to me for answers. Knowing the blueprint only existed in my head.

Every one of the band had begun honing their role. Theo was spending every second of his life with his bass. He'd snort speed just before we went on stage, said it helped him focus his playing. He didn't play bass like anyone else, but had this totally unique take. He'd caress the strings to make them vibrate. Backstage Jack would drum furiously onto his knees, wanting to build his strength so that his opening salvo shook the audience. Simon would stand with his head back, looking up at the ceiling.

Top Of The Pops was just a puppet show. It was the next gig that made me think we could truly change people. Some left their jobs without taking leave to travel to see us. Zipping each other up, then walking out into a stinging circle of orange light. The throbbing background track grinding in my ear, the crowd giving out this hungry roar.

I'd watched how crowds danced at gigs. The same, mechanical movements they fell into. Allowing themselves a tiny bit of self-expression for a few moments. But I was going to shake them out of their suburban stupor.

Onstage, the three others looked over at me for the signal to start. I'd *get a taste in my mouth and nod to Jack, who'd start pounding out this tribal drum tattoo. Theo twisting himself into shapes, trying to work a bass line around it. Simon, bent over his pedals, ready to unleash weird science.*

As a singer there's always this second when you go to the mike and you have no idea what's going to come out. I was shaking then, wondering if I'd be found out. The crowd looking up at me, needing something. On a good night you get caught in the flow, all the worries vanish. This dark poison wells up in you and you just have to ease it out through your mouth.

That was what happened that night, for the first time.

It hit hard.

The band kicked in and I was seized by this neurotic energy. It was so powerful. As my voice filled the room it vibrated my body, the deep tone coming out of my mouth scaring even me. All the bodies started moving, pogo-ing. Trying to adjust, find a way through the chaos. They were all hemmed in for the next hour, forced into this small coup. They had to make sense of it, one by one.

Gradually I knew they'd start to think. And realize, this is something real.

There's this elation when hundreds of slender women sing your words back at you. Their bodies trying to adjust to something you've made.

That night I felt such devotion to my band. I couldn't believe we'd got to this point so quickly, where we could floor audiences. Just flatten them.

I would have done anything for my band then. Simon unleashing these rolling fields of sound. Theo creating this constant pulse under it all. Jack driving us forward. A team.

We built and built and built. We took the audience to new planes, into weird annexes they didn't know their minds possessed. Brutally confronted them with themselves.

As the last song crashed to its knees the lights gradually dimmed, until all that was left was a final note in the darkness. A huge full stop.

The audience standing stunned. Trying to process what'd just happened.

When the lights came back on the stage was empty, the four of us stood in the wings. The crowd gave out this roar that shook the ceiling, and we looked at each other, our eyes wide with fear and pleasure and expectation. Our hearts thundering.

During the gig I'd seen Bonny in the wings, holding a fan of backstage passes. As the last notes of the concert rang out I saw her go out into the crowd, hand them out to some of the younger women. Mostly ones dressed like fans, with fur-trimmed leather and hairspray, this mix of perfume and perspiration that filled me with excitement. She directed them backstage, where journalists were mingling. Like scum round a pan.

The back stage party was like a pressure cooker. The odour of roadies, just off Grateful Dead tours, mixing with the perfume of young girls in glittering heels. All of them congregating in the far corner, taking it in. I'd expected us to be too noisy, too strange to attract that crowd. I wondered if they would stay with us for long before moving onto the next new boys, with their songs about discos and bedsits.

I found a beer and somewhere to sit on the side as more and more girls seeped in. Until the room was this big, seductive tide of bracelets and lip-gloss. Sparkling and swaying.

I took a swig, tried to pick out Simon. The girls looked hesitant, cautious. Every now and again they snapped into action. Consulted with a mate, dressed identically but with a different necklace, before running over to the table of drinks. Seconds later they'd be back at their mate's side, giving a snap verdict. Standing there, arms folded. Watching again.

In come the journalists. College boys with tape recorders slung over one tweed shoulder. Lank hair, darkened by sunless years. Trying to make contact with these girls.

As I drank, I felt people staring at me. I listened in to one of the girls talking to Theo. 'You were so amazing,' she said. 'We hitched a ride all the way down from Liverpool just to see you.'

'We have nowhere to stay,' another said.

Theo nodded. 'We're all homeless, when the lights go up,' he said. But her friends weren't listening. They were looking at the cut of his leather jacket, wondering where he'd bought it from.

'Is it true you're dating that girl from The Passions?'

'Is it true your jacket is from Sex?'

But he never gave a specific answer. He just responded with gin. Whatever the question was, he'd say 'Here, have a drink.'

Pop stars don't cater, they make a canvas.

It's pretty much their only job.

No one tried to speak to me. They looked at me, but didn't come close. I was told I used to give off this negative force-field then.

Not like Theo.

Simon came over and rolled a joint at my side. Bonny said 'You can't smoke that in here, what if the press see?' Simon laughed.

'Come on,' she said. 'Presentation, presentation, presentation.'

'You serious, Bon?'

She lowered her voice.

'Yes, I'm deadly serious, Simon. Every music paper has sent someone here tonight. Don't give them a reason to turn their back on you. The Grassmen are ready to steal your thunder as it is.'

The Grassmen were our support act. Four MIT students who used recorded factory sounds instead of drums.

Simon looked incredulous. 'That lot from Akron?'

'Yeah. Look at that. All the journalists are cornering them. Leaving you well alone.'

'They think Robert will chin them. No one will go near him.'

I drank. 'Don't be daft.'

'Well how come they're over there then?' Bonny asked me.

'Because they're courting the journalists right back, aren't they?' I said. 'We're not like that. You know how it works, Bon. Tell them what we're all about and they won't try to work it out for themselves.'

She smiled, waved her cocktail glass. 'Rubbish, Robert. You play hard to get at this stage and they'll just ignore you. You're not big *enough for those games. Someone's got to make it happen.'*

'You're on a hiding to nothing,' I said.

'I think he's right,' a voice said.

It was one of the ushers from the event, a girl with shining blonde hair. Bonny had introduced me to her on the way in. Told me to ask her for anything we needed. I'd been distracted during sound check by her, the way she nodded enthusiastically whenever I asked for something. Who am I to give orders to someone like her, I thought. I'm nothing.

'Right about what?' I asked.

'About not going after the journalists.' She dropped her voice. I noticed just how small she was. Gazelle-thin. Tiny shoulders. 'That band will be here today, gone tomorrow. I'd keep your distance. Get them to chase after you.'

Bonny walked off. I could see she thought her more a girl than a woman.

'Is that what you do?' I asked.

She blushed. 'I'm not chasing after anyone. I'm doing my job.'

I looked at the glass of wine in her hand. She laughed.

'Yeah, so what? I'm not on the clock anymore.'

Her eyelashes were almost too long for her face.

'So you thought you'd come backstage after your shift ended?'

'Yeah. See what's what. Why, was I not supposed to?'

'Course. And what do you think so far?'

We exchanged glances.

'It's a bit of a circus.'

'Bonny would have me schmoozing with everyone, like some politician,' I said, pointing out our manageress. We watched as she tried to prise herself between the radiation suits The Grassmen wore.

'You don't need to do that,' she said. 'But if a fan is desperate to talk to you, and you give them a few minutes...'

'What, like I am now?'

She laughed. 'I'm not a fan. I'm just doing my job.'

'Careful,' I said. 'I'm pretty sure some Nazis had that motto.'

She laughed.

'What did you think of our set?'

She looked down at her glass. It struck me that I didn't care what any of the girls in the corner thought. Only what the small girl in the gold cardigan said next.

'You did remind me of Iggy Pop,' she said.

'So what's your name?' I asked.

'Frankie.'

Nataly wrote her first letter to me soon after I'd met Frankie. It wasn't the best time to receive it.

My relationship with Frankie had moved fast, and somehow I already knew that one day she'd be my wife. I wouldn't propose romantically, and I wouldn't gradually woo her. But there'd been such a sense of importance around our early conversations that I knew marriage was inevitable. She found a place in my daily routine so quickly, started taking up chores. Before that Bonny had been the only one who'd shown concern about the way I lived. Who reminded me to eat, and told me off if I picked at my arm with a knife or a compass when we all watched TV. I reckon Bonny felt put out at the way Frankie took over. Bonny had found me a decent place to live, got me sleeping properly, and now here was this stranger running the show. Before long she was at my place every night. Had her feet well under the table. But it felt good, in a way, to have someone want to nurture me.

The band was making waves and I only had the occasional day off. I'd use them to hang around at the offices of Exit Discs. There was a girl in the design department who wore Buddy Holly glasses, who'd show me her artwork for our next single. Sleek flyovers and underpasses. Then our A&R man would hand me a sack full of mail and I'd pick through it. But Nataly's letter had been sent to Bonny. She made a point of handing it to me when she dropped by.

'Who's it from?' I said.

'Someone who didn't trust giving it to a man. Worth a read, I'd say.'

I sat on the window sill and watched Bonny mount her moped

outside. *Normally I read letters from fans with an outstretched arm. You don't take it on, the praise. Reading between the lines, they always want something. And the compliments don't ring true. They've bought into the myth that's been pushed and think they're dealing with that.*

This letter was different.

It was written neatly in black ink. Not the usual green. She apologised for bothering me, admitted she had little idea why she was writing. Said she was an Athenian girl in her late twenties who wanted to jack in the life she'd started. Start again as a musician.

She couldn't play a note, she said. Wasn't even sure she could carry a tune in a bucket. But she'd listened to Siouxie Sioux and now she didn't know what to do with the emotion. I knew how that felt.

I kept reading.

She'd just jacked in her a job in marketing and had formed a band. She'd bought my first single and got Bonny's address off her company ad in Melody Maker.

I'm not after a support slot, she wrote. I'm not trying to sleep with you. I don't even want you to listen to the songs I'm working on. But your last single did something to me. And I want to know how you did it.

The letter was like a manifesto. Grids of anger, laced with strychnine.

She asked specifics. 'How did you find like-minded people? How do you get started? How can I get to the point where I can change people?' It tailed off quickly. It ended with 'You won't write back.'

I wrote back the next day. From then on, whenever I saw Bonny, she'd have another letter to give me. She never told Nataly to send it to my home address, and she never minded playing courier.

I think she thought Nataly was better for me than Frankie. An artist who'd challenge me. She always wanted a finger in every pie, Bonny.

In later letters Nataly would get too dark. You could sense her trying to articulate something. Bad poetry crept in, stuff about 'black rivers' and 'fingers of darkness'. Mentions of obscure Italian film directors no one knew. I started to mention my own obsessions. How I dreamt about shining cars and ruined cities. We started trading internal furniture. The pieces that only mean something to you. You can't do that with many people, so you protect the ones you can exchange with. Keep them for yourself.

We kept on writing while I was on tour, and I kept it quiet. I'd tell her how the shows went, what I'd learnt, what I feared. What I was reading. Burroughs, Crowley. She'd then read the same books, in some dark flat in London, with the blinds down. Making notes. Then she'd write back. Pushing me.

Romance never crept in, but we both knew we were on intimate ground. You don't lay yourself out like that without being vulnerable. She was so disciplined about replying, it was like she was doing a course by mail order. If I was late she'd want to know why. What is this, I thought?

We'd been writing for about two months when she sent a photo of herself. It was a clipping of her onstage at her first gig, taken from the local newspaper. Dark, slanted fringe covering most of her face as she focused on her guitar. A slim, Greek girl in a black dress. Trying to put a song across to a room full of indifferent strangers. Men looking at her thighs and her breasts. Not listening.

'How do you make them sit up and take notice?' she asked. 'How do you tell them that you're not messing about, and you will be heard?'

I drew a map of my movements onstage. Zones that I moved in. Make your own set of rules, I said. Exhilarate them by teaching them what they are during a show.

She tried it out. Then wrote to me again. 'Come and see me live,' she said. 'See what you think.'

Her next gig was at some pub in Islington. The Hope and Anchor. I told Frankie I was going out with Bonny. Bonny took me for a pint over the road but then left well before the gig. I remember thinking, 'you know what you're doing'.

Outside the pub a punter guided his dog to a dish of stale water. I had on a black raincoat, collar pulled up. A toothless punk still recognised me, and nodded slowly. I nodded back, and as I went inside I heard him shout, 'Did you see who that was?'

I took my pint inside the venue. Grim. This stench of pies and trapped fag smoke. Tinny drums pummelling through the speakers.

The ceiling was low and sweat seeped off the walls. Every inch covered in graffiti, promoting this or that band. People's dreams, piled up like wrecked cars. It was filling fast and I couldn't see Nataly anywhere. Three women in black jeans with shredded t-shirts were bringing amps down the stairs. A woman with a severe, dark haircut following behind, carrying a bunch of leads. Scanning the faces.

I caught her eye and smiled. She didn't smile back. Showed them where to stack the amps. I leant against the bar.

When she went on stage, in front of the microphone stand, she held both her arms out, straining her finger-tips. Then she said to her bassist, 'Don't come any nearer than that.'

She stuck a set-list to the floor with masking tape. As she crouched down I saw there was nothing under her short, strappy black dress. A tiny gash of dark hair under her armpits. Sharp black heels. When she stood up I could see she had no makeup on. Her features were so strong that already men were clamouring at the front in a tight semi-circle, tightening. Looking everywhere but at her. She saw it and leant into the mike. 'I'd like to invite the women in the audience to come to the front,' she said.

One or two did, nodding to themselves.

'You're Robert Wardner,' someone shouted. I looked round. A man, laughing, stumbled over to me. Pretending someone had pushed him.

He looked up at me, jabbing his forefingers alternately. 'You're Robert Wardner,' he repeated.

'What do you want?'

'Have you come to see Diameter?'

'No. Them.' I said, nodding at the stage.

'Are you shagging her?'

I put the glass down, went to his nose. Intakes of breath all around. 'Do you want to get fucking knocked out?' I said.

Nataly was coiling a mike lead onstage.

'Robert Wardner's here!' someone shouted.

I leant back on the bar, hoping Nataly hadn't seen.

'Let him be,' said the soundman.

A lot of people around me were hunched, looking into their glasses. I wanted to smash a few heads against the bar. I focused.

Now it was all about me, not her.

I looked at the sea of hunched shoulders. Everyone still, now. Nataly looked at them too, and then for the first time that night she smiled.

She likes tension too, I thought. It fuels her.

Nataly had something about her.

As the drummer pounded out a rhythm she threw shards of untreated guitar over it. When she sang, her head bobbed up and down, like a coach talking to a boxer. Between songs the younger members looked to her and were instructed with a glance.

Before the last song there was a moment when she held out her hands and slowly flexed them into fists. The drummer, watching her, began to make thuds on the bass drum in time with it. She started to speak. 'I want you to take all your poison, and dance it out in this song.'

I sensed people straining to catch every word. 'There's a beat,' she said, snapping her fingers at the drummer. 'And there's a tune. And in the chorus, the words. 'This is where I let my poison out.' Now are you going to sing it with me or not?'

A few cheers. From somewhere at the back, a woman wailed. Cracked open, at last.

'I said, are you going to sing it with me or not? I'm not here for the fun of it.'

'Yeah!' a man shouted, raising his pint.

Her splintering guitar line bled into a raw chorus. 'This is where I let my poison out,' she sang. Stamping her feet to every syllable.

In waves, the audience sang it back. Streaks of devotion fizzling through them. It built.

By the end, I had the mantra under my skin. She was crashing the neck of her guitar against the mike stand in time, letting it ring out its hollow plea. Backed with echoing drums. 'This is where I let my poison out.'

They chanted it back. It was like a political rally. Fists in the air. She was evangelical. 'This is where I let my poison out.'

On the final note, some of them screamed their throats raw.

At the bar after, she gave me a tight grin. She reached over the counter and pulled out a bottle. 'You made it then,' she said.

'You followed my instructions,' I said. Her dress clung to her body. A patch of skin above her breasts glistening with sweat.

'Guidelines,' she answered. 'No one instructs me.'

We had dinner.

Despite all those letters, it was still like walking on a tightrope to get to that point. She suggested a cheap Italian place. We barely looked at each other when she ordered salad and water. It was only once we were left well alone that she wanted to talk. As she asked her first question her knife was suspended in the air. 'How did you learn to perform?'

I watched the blade glimmer. 'It's not a performance,' I said. 'You're just a conduit.'

'For what?'

'For everything the audience can't put across themselves.'

'But how do you know what they want to express?'

I looked her in the eye. 'You knew. It's at the back of the room. Lingering over their heads. Resentment, bitterness, rejection. You tap into it.'

'What about if none of that is there? If there's only apathy?'

'Apathy's just a front. People offer it when there's something stronger hiding underneath. You have to work harder to tap into it, but then your performance has even more power.'

She'd listen, then cut and eat. Gradually, the knife was laid down. She weaved her fingers. 'There was something at the end there, that finally made me feel right.' The hard eyes softened. 'I could learn so much from you.'

'Soon, I'll be learning from you.'

'True,' she said.

At the end she wrote her phone number on the receipt. When we left she clasped her fingers on my coat for a second, and looking at the floor she told me to 'go safe'.

I kept the phone number in a shoebox under my bed, along with a review I found of that gig. Whenever I saw Bonny I'd ask if she'd heard anything.

Some months I'd get nothing. I'd see a review in the NME, six or seven lines. They got bigger once she was signed. Eventually a letter would come, Bonny handing it to me with a smile.

'I've been in a black hole,' she'd write. There'd be so many apologies, so many obstacles, I could barely find Nataly in the writing. Sometimes the letters would stop and I'd think, that's it, she's gone. I'd write again, ask if she was alright. She'd say, 'Course I am.'

I'd say, 'What was all that about?'

She'd say, 'Forget it.' Every now and then we'd talk on the phone and towards the end she'd say the odd thing. Like 'Sometimes it's best if you keep your distance from me. I could be too much for you.'

'I'm not going to desert you if it gets a bit rough. This life you and I are making. It's not a merry-go-round.'

'You think you've been in some bad places, you don't know what my mind is capable of.'

'Don't be daft,' I'd say. 'What's the worst you could do to me?'

That number stayed in the box. I left her name off it. Just in case.

Melody Maker Reviews
December 21st, 1981

Hope And Anchor
Joyless seriousness aside, Diameter are saved by sheer firepower, and glamorous support.

Audiences don't come more puritanical than this. We're in punk territory here. Elvis Costello himself was seen propping up the bar for a pint of snakebite a week back. Now it's Transit Record's new signing **Diameter** who're taking the stage. Few in number but determined in taste, the local punks sit resolutely at the back, adopting an impress-me stance. Frankly, if **Diameter** can impress here, nothing can stop them.

But first, there's **Rosary.** With some stripped-back punk rock as puritanical as their name suggests and a singer who is – yikes!- a girl. A young girl at that. Siouxie Sioux with more Penguin Paperbacks than she knows what to do with. Scrubbed of all makeup, serious as an off-duty ballerina. Fronting a band who rock like her neglected younger siblings, vying for attention.

No doubt that's a comparison set to haunt singer Nataly Callis. All sharp stares and sharper stilettos, she's the female dictator that you hope refuses to yield. At the end she has us all marching to her tune. A perfect storm of brittle guitar, angular poses and a gut-shaking vox. Watch this space for more...

After all that, **Diameter** take their time to impress. Frontman Alex McGregor doesn't have an iota of Callis' charm, and you're left praying for the arrival of a riff that'll set The Starship **Diameter** on course for the heart of the sun. A hope that fades when he introduces himself with the words 'We're from Birmingham. But can you forgive us?'

Faux-naivety aside, **Diameter** are redeemed by the sheer force of their sound. They smash through their stage set with just the right degree of willful abandon, suggesting that those recent Cure records have not been neglected by the Brummie set. In the brilliant 'Fingers In Ears' the keyboardist unleashes a wall of fire that almost satisfies your hunger for a magnificent riff. It's a more meat-and-potatoes set than **Rosary** offer, certainly. But as McGregor circles the stage like a caged tiger, mesmerized by the exertions of his band, it is almost as exciting. To screams of feedback, **Diameter** rumble nosily to an end, and London's punk mafia pat each other on the back for a night out well done.

2

Sam got off the tube at Shoreditch, resisting the offers of free newspapers as he struggled to follow the instructions on a crumpled printout. The pictures on the publisher's website had suggested he was heading into a business empire, with various different wings. But having arrived at a cramped alley off the main road, he instead found himself having to search for mere clues. Fragments of the company's aesthetic, hinted at on their lurid website.

Behind posters hurriedly pasted to walls there were few street numbers visible. Did Mason House only exist online, he wondered? Lost beneath more recent ideas? Consulting the map, Sam reasoned that it had to be somewhere between the stall selling genuine Jamaican jerk chicken at his side and the messy mobile phone shop at the end.

A sign indicated that the publishers owned the building glistening by an array of phone covers. Outside it, music played from a ghetto blaster encrusted with glitter.

As he walked through the glass entrance Sam saw a semi-circle of staff taking turns to blast graffiti onto a wooden panel. 'Mason House' it said. 'The future they promised us.' Sam giggled, unable to supress his derision.

He offered his name to a woman with a pierced lip at the front desk, and asked where he might find Martin Graham. 'Hi Sam, yes, Martin is expecting you,' she said, reaching for the intercom. 'Mart, Sam is here.'

'Great. Send him up,' the voice replied.

She led Sam up a sticky set of steel steps at the back of the room, into an open-plan office on the first floor. Martin was a lean man with a thatch of wiry hair, and a jutting jaw. He somehow worked amongst a circle of blow-up furniture. Framed prints of book covers surrounded him on the walls. Culture slimed over him from all sides, demanding excessive praise.

'This is Martin,' the woman said, extending her hand. Martin instantly flipped down the lid of his laptop. He tore off his designer glasses and rose to greet Sam.

'Sam! It was good of you to come. I hope you didn't travel all the way down just for this?'

'Er, no. Not at all. I was down for other business as well.'

'Wonderful.'

Sam found himself being steered onto a beanbag, on which he struggled to stay upright. Women with bright red lips and insolent expressions tapped at computers. Martin saw Sam taking it all in, and smiled. 'Can we get you a drink at all? We have a blender somewhere in the office. Polly can whip us up a mean smoothie.' A woman in a spotted headscarf rose, somewhat joylessly, at the mention of her name.

'An orange juice would be fine.'

'Amazing.'

'Can I get you anything, Martin?' Polly asked.

'I'll have a skinny caramel frappuccino with the chocolate space-dust,' he said, twirling his fingers. His eyes rested on Sam, expectant and suspicious.

'So. What have you got for me?'

Sam tried to remember his notes, but his mind went blank. A woman wearing a sailor hat pushed a pencil into a whirring machine, and Sam gritted his teeth. 'There are forums about The National Grid online that have gone into overdrive with the rumours that Wardner's going to make a return. They didn't even know if he was alive. When he vanished people assumed it was suicide, but his family were always so sure he would never have done that.'

'So these fans are not put off by this talk that he might be a murderer?'

'I don't think they believe he could be.'

'I hear that he developed this intense relationship with a fan of his. She wouldn't let him out of her sight so he drove down to the coast with her. Stabbed her in his car and then threw her body off a cliff.'

'That story is the reason he's never stayed out of the papers for very long. But there was never a body, so I don't know how that could be true.'

Martin leaned back on his chair, and started squeezing a small stuffed toy.

'Could it have been washed away? What about the head of his record label, this Andrew Cunningham? I was told him and Wardner had a big blow out and Cunningham was found dead not long after. Could there be something in that?'

Sam shook his head. 'There was a lot about Cunningham's death in the papers at the time. But the coroner's verdict was Cunningham died of a heart attack. Wardner wasn't implicated.'

'But then why did he vanish?'

'Well no one even knows where Wardner went,' Sam said, sitting up. 'There is a market for this story. I still have all the contacts from the early years, and I've stayed on top of the case as it's developed. It's been a bit of a preoccupation of mine. I could interview those closest to him, all in the course of tracking him down. Then get his side of the story, write it up. I really think...' He gulped. Was he really going to say these words? 'I really think that Mason House could be sitting on the biggest music news story of the next decade.'

That was terrible, Sam thought. I've blown it.

Martin laughed. 'I don't know about that. But of course, I'm curious. Otherwise I wouldn't have called. I think we could make this happen.' As he smiled Sam noticed a rather sharp set of incisors.

Behind Sam, someone coughed.

'Ah, yes,' Martin said. 'Sam, I'd like you to meet the person whose been pushing this story down at my end. Camille.'

He raised his eyes as a slender, dark-haired woman stepped

forward. As she looked up he saw she had brooding, finely cut features. She wore a white vintage lace dress, with a blue bow in her hair.

'Camille, this is Sam,' Martin said. Sam noticed Camille's face had vulnerability, as if it could express any emotion at just a moment's notice. As she leant forward to shake his hand Sam had the sense she wasn't aware of the potency of her presence.

'I'm glad you came down,' she said. 'I was worried this book was going to be pie-in-the-sky.'

Sam laughed. Her voice was an unusual combination of accents. The soft, creamy vowels of a Parisian blended with a touch of recent Cockney.

'No, I'm going to pull that pie right out of the sky,' he said.

She laughed. 'I don't know if Martin has told you,' she said, 'but I used to read all of your columns in the weeklies when I was at school. I loved your character studies of Robert. I think you really got what he was about.'

'I'm glad you think so,' he replied.

'I read all your articles on The National Grid again when I was preparing a brief for Martin,' she continued. 'Have you never thought about releasing them as a collection?'

'No, I haven't,' Sam said, rubbing his neck. 'But if you were instrumental in getting Martin interested in the story I should probably thank you.' He found himself taking on the rhythms of her voice.

'Only if you manage to escape unscathed,' Martin said.

'I don't believe he was a murderer,' Camille replied. She stood upright, and clasped her hands against her hips. 'How could he go from *Top Of The Pops* to cold-blooded murder in a year?'

Martin made eye contact with Sam. 'Let's hope he didn't, for Sam's sake.'

'It would just break my heart to even think that he was a killer,' Camille said. 'When I was a girl, he was one of the few people who seemed to speak about the truth of the modern world. I used to read him talking about Manchester, and their club scene, and it made me think England must be so exotic!'

'That's great. That's just great,' Martin said, looking between them. 'Now, where is that file I had for Ivan? We put together a budget for this guy to write a book on his hunt for Banksy, and I see no reason why we can't work with the same numbers.'

'Great.'

He leant over a computer on the corner of his desk and clicked a few times, before walking over to the printer as it spewed out a page. He handed it to Sam.

'As you can see,' Martin said, 'we'll give you £1500 just to get you on your way, and that should be more than enough to fund your first few weeks of research. Do some interviews with the key players from Wardner's life. Whoever will lead you to him. He'll need to be tracked down by the final deadline to release the final payment, which is obviously the biggest.'

'It's okay. I can do this full-time.'

'For one and a half grand?'

I would need to find Wardner straight away, Sam thought. The money would cover the first mortgage payment. He could go back to Elsa with his head held high, just.

'Can you live with that?'

'Of course. I'm itching to get started.'

Polly came back into the room, with a plastic flask of orange juice and a glass of elaborately decorated milky fluid. 'Thanks, Polly,' Martin said.

'That's so exciting,' Camille said, her eyes on the piece of paper. 'And if you are lucky enough to be able to speak with Wardner you must phone and let me know what he's like straight away.'

'If I survive it.'

'I wouldn't be brave enough to try and track him down.'

'Sounds like you know as much about his work as I do?'

'Maybe. Wardner's records meant the world to me,' she said.

'I grew up in Paris and had those terrible teenage years. Bullied at school, always trying to hide. Just lived in records, that sort of thing. Spent a week inside 'Tainted Love'.'

'That must have been cramped,' Martin said.

'Bit pretentious, isn't it, to live that way?'

'No, I don't think so,' Sam said.

'Anyway,' she answered, blushing. 'Here's my business card, Sherlock. If you ever need a Dr. Watson, you know where to find me.'

'Thanks,' Sam said. He fished a scrap piece of paper from his pocket, and receiving a pen from Martin, scrawled out his numbers for her. 'I could do with those too,' Martin said. 'We got your new number off a journalist who used to work with you, and we weren't even sure it was right.'

'Tristan?' Sam didn't let on he was the only friend he still had in that world.

Martin nodded, finishing his drink nosily. 'I can see that I'm going to struggle to keep Camille on task now, Sam. You have her all fired up.'

Camille looked Sam up and down. 'He does indeed,' she said.

ROBERT WARDNER

Twenty three years of my life had been leading to this moment. I was about to start recording my debut album.

It felt a bit like being a teenager, when every moment seemed important, permanent.

We were booked into a wood-panelled recording studio out in the Hertfordshire countryside. As we pulled into the drive in a battered Volvo an ashen-faced Robert Plant was leaving, flanked with his entourage. We hadn't had our advance through yet so all our instruments were still in bin bags. When Theo moved to pull his bass out the back seat Simon pulled him back.

'What are you doing?' Theo asked.

'What I'm doing is preventing Led Zeppelin from seeing that we still use black bin liners to transport our instruments.'

'So what if he sees?'

Theo was mad for it, never cared what people thought.

Simon watched big-haired musos pass in front of the car, before turning to Theo. 'That's going to look good in Smash Hits, *isn't it Theo? When a reporter asks them, 'Did you meet any other bands while you were recording,' and Robert Plant goes 'No, but a group of dustmen in skin-tight leather were mincing inside when we left'.'*

'It's the eighties,' I said. 'We're taking over from them.'

I watched as Plant pushed his hands into his leather jacket and made his way to a Mercedes.

'We can't hang about in here all day,' Jack said.

'That's right,' I said. 'We have got work to do.'

Through the car windscreen we saw Bonny advancing towards us, in a huge fur coat. She opened the door.

'Get out the car,' she said. 'What are you waiting for?'

Simon started to move.

'We've entered the big league now,' she said, as we unloaded. There was a tremor in her voice. She couldn't stop grinning. She knew it was

only a matter of time before she became famous herself, now.

Bonny loved moments like this. Lived for them.

It was only when we were inside that I stopped feeling like a joke. I realized something special was about to happen. Standing in that performance space. My lyrics scrawled out in front of me.

A few inches from me, Simon was on his knees, adjusting his bank of pedals. Theo, jumping like a grass hopper, headphones falling off his head. Jack, twirling drum sticks. His left knee bouncing.

I looked round, through the screen separating us from our producer, Vicente.

Exit Discs hadn't been able to arrange it. It was Bonny who pulled that off. In the last five years Vicente had turned countless amateurs into platinum-selling, critically acclaimed artists. What's more, he'd agreed to do it for half the price when he heard our demo. Sent a postcard to Bonny with the words, 'I'm speechless.'

He stood behind the screen in outsized sunglasses, chest hair poking through gold medallions. Bonny behind him, biting her nails.

You realize then that everyone's looking at you. The vision they're all wanting to come to life only exists in your head. It's on that crumpled piece of paper in front of you.

You've convinced them you can do it. You can't screw up.

Vicente came on the intercom. You and him have prepared for this moment for weeks. You've stayed up all night in his Kensington mansion, in the kind of house you never knew existed. Trying to work out arrangements for your songs with one finger, on his grand piano in a huge white room. Him standing there with a pair of scissors, shredding your lyrics and rearranging them. Burroughs' cut-up technique. Rasping, with his weird blend of Italian and Estuary the words, 'We'll keep it raw. You'll all play it live.'

You've sat with a Mini-Moog in his front room while his Yugoslavian supermodel wife offers you canapés, your lyrics about a decaying Britain bristling up at you. You've talked until the small hours about what this record means to you. How you don't care about the luxury, how you just want to create the perfect cry for help. You've told him how you feel about Thatcher, about the recession. How angry it makes you. He's seen the 'Britain Isn't Working' posters and he talks about Mussolini, post-war Italy. He tells you to be careful of your twenties. Tells you they're a tightrope.

Arriving in the studio, you've lain on the sofa in the reception suite, trying to imagine how the record will sound. Bonny's stood over you, put her hand on your shoulder and told you to make it good. Both of you knowing this is your only chance of making a better life for yourselves.

All of that, leading up to this moment.

Vicente clears his throat. 'Gentlemen, 'A State Of Exile' first,' he shouts. 'Four counts, Jack, and we'll drop you in.'

Simon looks round us all. 'Right, keep them eyes up lads,' he says.

Vicente raises a finger. You close your eyes.

A moment later the synths fill your ears. They're soon pinned back by the opening attack from Jack's drums, blasting your jeans against your legs. Even with your eyes closed you can still make out Theo's silhouette. He arches over his bass. Attacking the two-note riff that creates a canvas for Simon.

Vicente is frantically waving from the control booth, motioning to Simon to improvise for a few bars.

Simon doesn't need prompting. He's forgotten the plot long ago, and when his plectrum strikes the strings it's not the soothing cloud you're all expecting, but a jagged stab of noise. He bends over his guitar, jerking the tremolo arm. Throws his head back. Theo's knocked sideways as Simon strikes the strings above the nut of the guitar, unleashing a brittle shower of shards. Theo's bass line then combining with his own, drill-like imitation. Then Simon stamps on a pedal and that familiar sound emerges. He turns to you, one foot on the pedal, and snaps it off.

You open your mouth.

You don't even need to look at the lyric sheet.

You're inside the sleek world of paranoia and high rises that you've created in your head.

Your voice gives out for the final chorus, but Vicente is still jumping at the end. 'That was what we needed,' he shouts.

Bonny comes on the intercom. 'We happy?'

Jack nods enthusiastically. Theo agrees, glad no one noticed his mistake in the third bridge. Simon looks to you.

'Rob?'

'I kept sitting under the note in the chorus,' you say. 'Sounded like a flat tyre.'

'Nah, you didn't.'

Vicente catches your comment on the intercom. 'Very well, he says. 'We'll go again. Until you happy, Robert.'

Before the track begins again you just catch Bonny whispering in Vicente's ear. 'What was wrong with that?' she asks him.

'Nothing,' he says.

3

Sam drove with his body close to the wheel until he found the junction for the A40, gasping open amongst the grey backdrop.

He fiddled with the stereo; irritated that Elsa wasn't with him to share in this moment. Joy Division's 'Disorder' reverberated around the car's interior, the hard surfaces of the city replaced now by the hard surfaces of the song.

He knew Elsa's mind would automatically look for cracks in his story. At that moment he missed the Elsa he had first met.

During his first year in halls Elsa had lived at the end of his corridor. Sam had spent that time feeling intoxicated by the idea that he could become a music journalist. Few people in the halls seemed to share his artistic preoccupations, preferring instead to dress up variously as gladiators, schoolgirls and sperm, for the rag week. The only students who were interested in serious subjects carried around copies of Sartre and pinned up pictures of Bobby Sands in their rooms. But Sam couldn't bring himself to speak to them.

It was a relief when a girl in the flat opposite invited him and a friend over for a Halloween party. As they both sat amongst the broken fairy lights and charred cupcakes, Sam noticed a girl on the windowsill, her arms around her knees. She had blonde, almost white hair held back by a glittering red clip. Her face was whitened with powder and her eyes blackened, both accentuating her smudged scarlet lipstick. She looked straight at Sam.

During the party everyone delivered fragments of their past as though they were unbearably precious. It seemed to be the only skill people learnt at university, a technique that real life would stifle the use of. An American girl was passionately talking about the effect Kennedy getting shot had on the US. 'The bullet symbolised a society who will no longer raise celebrities above ideas,' she said. Elsa took a cap gun from the table and mimed blowing her head off. She acted out imaginary streams of blood pouring onto the floor.

At the end of the party Sam found himself stooped over her guitar in her kitchen. She made him teach her the chords to David Bowie's 'Starman'.

The journey from the ruined kitchen to her bedroom remained smeared in his memory. It seemed inevitable even as it happened, like watching a curious object lap its way to the shore. As she sat opposite him on the bed, under a Marc Bolan poster, she flicked through her journal. His eyes caught mentions of flirtations, sequins, and nightclubs. He wished that he could be sat behind her, feasting on the details. She didn't meet his eye as she closed the book and put it back in a drawer. In the weeks that followed Sam became familiar with the aching morning light of her bedroom, and the snatched sentiments within that book. One day, she swore, she'd shape them into songs.

A thin sheet of rain peppered the car window, and Sam bolted to attention. He thought how Elsa had changed over the years. In the early days that journal had represented a fertile ground between them, which he had hoped would one day open into an artistic life. Was it his fault that that vision hadn't ever been realized?

A little further north he signalled off for Knutsford Services, just before the looming J19. He parked outside the Burger King.

Just entering the complex, Sam felt that he had entered the kind of urban wilderness which Wardner had probably vanished into. His songs were full of tower blocks and cityscapes, and Sam had no doubt that he might well have retreated into such a hinterland. At that moment he understood the pull of them too, the dark thrill of leaving your identity at the car and joining the drifting bodies. Surely such abandonment was the first stage in creating a new identity?

He sluiced water across his face in the toilets. His reflection in the mirror was distorted by the warped glass. These places restyle us, he thought. Wardner could look completely different by now, if he took their lead.

Outside, as he queued at Burger King, a man ordering food at the counter caught Sam's attention. There was something about his forward lean that evoked Wardner. A chill arose on the back of Sam's neck and he found himself tensing, waiting furiously for the man to turn.

But the man wouldn't let Sam see his face. He remained stiffly upright, facing straight ahead, sidestepping once he had his food to a table by the counter, where he kept his back to Sam.

Sam ate his own food with his eyes trained on the man's back. Why did he remind him of Wardner so much? It can't be him, Sam thought.

Sam focused on his limp sandwich, and when he rose a few minutes later he was frustrated to see the man had gone. He wiped his mouth, shoved the tray into a rack and made his way back to his car.

He drove out of the car park, easing onto the slip road. He was just looking down the motorway for a gap when a white transit van loomed into his rear view mirror. It was bearing down on him, fast. Sam expected him to brake. But the driver clearly had no intention of slowing. It was going to smash into him. Panicking, Sam released the clutch and pumped the accelerator. His car skidded away. But the van kept coming, and Sam had to speed onto the motorway. But he'd been pushed in front of a huge articulated lorry. It blasted its hooter as it towered over Sam, dwarfing his car as he felt himself disappear under it. Sam floored the accelerator, the car jerking madly to one side. But the lorry driver kept his hooter down, and Sam was barely able to grip the wheel as he tried to get away. Awkwardly, he overtook two cars before slowing, easing onto the hard shoulder and putting his head on the wheel.

It took a very long time for his racing heart to stop. For the dark chill in his veins to settle.

But it wasn't the near-collision that had started him shaking. When he'd looked in the mirror to catch a glimpse of the van driver, he was sure it was Robert Wardner that was staring back at him.

ROBERT WARDNER

I charged out of the chair and with one lunge grabbed Cunningham by the neck and pinned him to the wall.

'Robert,' Bonny shouted, getting up.

'You won't win behaving like this,' Cunningham said, smiling as he wriggled about. I could feel the muscles tighten in his neck.

'You southerners love the sound of your own voices don't you?' I said, looking into his eyes. 'But you just can't tell when enough's enough.'

'Rob,' Bonny repeated, putting her hand on my shoulder. 'Put him down.'

'Better do what your babysitter says,' Cunningham whispered.

After a few more seconds of letting him squirm I released him from my grip, watching him pretend not to be shaken as he waddled back to his chair.

His solicitor went over to check on him. 'Are you alright?'

Cunningham nodded.

'So we can add attempted assaulted to the crib sheet then,' he said.

'What do expect?' Bonny snapped. 'You're threatening to steal music off four working class men from Manchester, who've been busting a gut trying to make a record for you. You expect things not to get nasty?'

'I expect them to understand that what I say goes.'

'I know you don't care what people think of you, Andrew. I can tell that from your waistcoat. But don't you think you could offer a little leeway? You've driven them to this point.'

We'd been deadlocked with the label for months. The clever dicks had decided that today's negotiations should ideally take place in an airless boardroom, until everyone was so knackered they could barely breathe. All I could hear was overhead fans, distant lifts.

All eyes were on me as I moved back to my seat at the end of the table. Simon was next to me, head in his hands. Next to us was our lawyer, who seemed to have done nothing but tot up numbers and what have you. Probably calculating what we owed him, again and again. Reckon he was just running down the clock.

At the other end of the table was Andrew Cunningham, head of the label. A bloated man with a thatch of grey hair, his belly spewing over his large-buckled belt. Bonny once described him as 'Perfect for the eighties, because if he was only more concerned with himself he'd grow a shell.' I'd soon learnt that the chief weapon in his armoury was pretending we weren't getting to him. It drove me to new heights of anger. His solicitor sat on his left, looking portly and smug as a grocer surveying a fresh table of produce.

Before I lost it we'd been debating the release of our debut album. It had been recorded five times, in various studios with brilliant reputations and useless producers. I'd wanted our tracks to capture on record a futuristic world. A world that seemed enticing at first, but that was chaotic when you scratched the surface. I wanted us to make a debut album that woke people up to the realities of modern life. I wanted to be like the lunatic in Times Square, wearing a placard, shouting 'The end of the world is nigh.'

My ambitions were pretty straightforward. On side one of the album I wanted to dismantle the modern world. On side two I wanted to rebuild it again.

But not one of the five college dropout producers Exit Discs had given us had been able to help us do it. They all seemed to be called Todd, and they all seemed to be unable to stay away from their birds for long enough to turn in a decent shift. Even Vicente didn't cut it.

After four recordings of the album we were no closer to getting the sounds in my head and were way over budget. This was when Cunningham called and told us they were going to release an album out of the recorded sessions whether we liked it or not. Unless we consented to an album release they would sue us for the recording costs. They appointed their lawyers, and I had to start convincing the bank to give us a loan so we could have one. Theirs had read so many books that he'd started to believe some of them. Mine was a mate of my Dad's.

It was then that the late-night wrangling started.

We had been cooped up in that long, dimly-lit conference room for six bloody hours before I went for him. It had got the point where Cunningham's solicitor was trying to wear me down, again and again making exaggerated statements and then saying 'Can you refute that?'

I looked over at Bonny, wanting our lioness of a manager to spring. But her eyes were like pissholes in the snow.

I kept clenching my fists.

The grocer motioned at me, with hands like hams. Cunningham looked up and in a low voice said 'He's too stupid to refute anything.'

Until that point I had, in a perverse way, been enjoying the tension. As a kid, when a situation turned nasty, I used to train myself to think that I wanted it to be that way. I'd try and believe that the more negative it got the more exciting I found it. But this was too much. Cunningham's insult prompted me to act.

I hadn't thought it was possible for the atmosphere to get any worse. Cunningham nursing his neck like a kicked cat, his solicitor now having a whole new set of numbers to work with. Neither Bonny nor Simon even able to look at me. Our lawyer had gone mute. Always did, when it got tough.

'I don't know what to do,' their solicitor said, standing up. 'Neither side will back down.'

Simon sighed.

'Well. Won't any of you even say anything?'

'Yeah,' I said. 'I'll say something. People like you,' I jabbed my finger at Cunningham, and stood up, 'are the reason this album needed to be written in the first place. When you've got your salary, and your cosy little ivory tower, you're dead happy to spout off about artistic integrity and us getting there together. But the minute you're asked to back your promises up with some strength of character, you come apart. You say you love good music, but you can't listen to it that carefully if you treat people like this. We signed with you because you said you'd stick with us and help us make the album we know we have in us. Rush this thing out and it'll all be over in weeks. Out of anyone in this room,

a label head should be the one who knows what it takes to make a masterpiece.'

He smirked.

'But that's all you do, innit? Look away and smirk. Everything's a joke to you. There's no commitment. It's just all about what you can do to speed up getting your pay cheque so you can get even fatter on your golf course, dressing like a shit cowboy.'

'Robert,' Bonny said, wearily.

'It's the decadent south, innit, Bon? They want to give up at forty-five. It's people like you giving in, when they have the clout to make the world better, that are responsible for this mess. You're laughing, but you're Thatcher's wet dream.'

'Robert,' Bonny said.

'No Bonny, it winds me up. Bollocks to it, I'm not having my music put out by them.'

'This is all we get,' Cunningham said to his lawyer. 'Speeches about the dying of the light, and the occasional burst of violence.'

'You don't understand,' Simon said. 'He can't bring himself to agree to put this record out as it stands. No matter how much work he's done. And believe me, you'll never know how much blood and guts he's put into this record. Put this LP out before he's finished with it and you'll be destroying ten years of his life.'

'Then we're in a stalemate,' Cunningham said. 'We're going to have to release it without consent.'

I stood up. It was like I was sleepwalking as I moved over to the door. As I passed Simon I quickly nudged him on the shoulder. Bonny moved over to him, her eyes flashing up at me.

Cunningham looked up at me, bemused.

I wanted him to know I wasn't messing about. That he'd gone too far.

His car keys were in front of him, next to a glass of water. I grabbed them.

'What are you doing?' He started laughing again.

I walked out of the conference room, clenching them in my fist. I had been staring out the windows at the basement car park when the arguments got boring, and now I walked down to it. I heard Cunningham following. The grocer grabbed his papers and joined him, along with the other suits.

As part of our record deal I was given the use of a long, silver Mercedes. Bonny had known that one way to convince me to sign with Exit Discs would be to get them to offer me a beautiful car, and it had worked. For all my idealism, I couldn't resist. My Dad had never even touched one.

I could sense them all watching me in the doorway to the car park as I walked over to it. I slipped inside.

'Give my keys back,' he shouted.

I reversed out, turning the car to face them. Then I dangled his keys in the windscreen, before throwing them onto the front dashboard. I could see the sweat shining on his forehead as he stamped closer. I had his attention now.

I drove the car round so it faced the back wall of the car park. I activated the lights. They sprayed onto the far wall of the low-ceilinged car park. On each side, fading into the smear of the distance, were grey concrete pillars. There was no one else down here. Just the cars owned by everyone in the board-room, huddled, watching in the doorway.

Seeing how I would react. Curious about what I could actually do.

I decided to show them. Up there in the boardroom, they had power over me. Their contracts told them they were in charge. But down here, I held the reins. I was in charge of a great, glistening, saloon car.

When I was weak they trod me underfoot. Now I was going to respond in a language they might understand. Cunningham negotiated only in terms of money and possessions. I was going to hit him where it hurt.

I pumped the accelerator and it sighed to life. Felt the blood pulse through my body and down to my legs. I made the engine exhale in pleasure. Slid into second, tyres squealing in excitement as I coursed through the car park.

They clamoured around the entrance. Even Cunningham not daring *to walk further.*

'What is he doing?' I heard him shout.

On my first circuit of the car park I went as close to the far wall as I could. Arced the car round with one sweep of the wheel. The engine didn't miss a pulse as I levelled up, heading for the group of huddled suits in the doorway.

I'm going to kill him, I thought.

They spread out, Cunningham's solicitor throwing papers into the air.

I roared nearer. Pushed the car until it was just a few feet from Cunningham, before something in me moved and I carved it sharply round. Like a knife drawing out of flesh. Pumped the accelerator and surged back towards the far wall.

What would Bonny and Simon be thinking?

The back wall drew closer again. I was getting addicted to that feeling I got at the last moment, avoiding the wall. I was driving round and round the car park in tight circles, round and round and round until that buzz was overwhelming. The thrill of freaking them out grew too strong to resist. I knew that I was too tired to play this risky game with steel and concrete much longer. I knew that soon steel and concrete would win. I would not stop but my body was ready to give out at any second. Collapse.

Reality was not a concern. All I cared about was this game, this knife-edge. As long as the game endured I had them. All the contracts were useless down here.

At any moment I could destroy what they really cared about.

I had never felt blood pump harder through me. I followed the rhythm of the loudening and quietening engine. Have you ever felt that sensation in moments of fear? It's life blood. With every circuit of the car I was saying to them, this is all you are doing. Driving faster and faster in circles, round and round and round until your bodies give out, and you crash.

And then, at the very moment that thought fired through me, my body gave out.

I felt my brain shut down, my eyes force themselves to close. I had just swerved off the back wall of the car park and begun roaring back to the figures in the doorway.

I was going to crash. And if I couldn't make it to Cunningham I was going to take all of their cars with me. Those neatly arranged, gleaming objects. I eased the bumper of my car into Cunningham's Jaguar. Felt the whole chassis shake as I knifed into his solicitor's BMW, then felt the back of my car kick out.

The force surprised me. I threw the wheel around, into the rest of them.

Span out of control.

Towards the mezzanine. They spread like doves.

Seconds before hitting it, I blacked out.

4

I'll find their manager, Sam thought.

But the 'Bonny Crawford' that showed up online was not identified as a manager, but an 'artist'. She was mentioned in an article for an upcoming exhibition in London, the title of which instantly ensnared him. Leaning in, Sam began to read.

The Lost Robert Wardner

A timely new exhibition of paintings about mysterious National Grid frontman Robert Wardner opens this month in London.

By Cassie Baker
4th April

The story of Robert Wardner, who almost completed a masterpiece album before vanishing under a dark cloud, is one of the most intriguing in popular music.

Owen Hopkins, in his documentary *Dark Ages Manchester*, portrayed him as an influential figure on the eighties scene, who personified the punk ethos of 'not selling out.' Wardner's voracious consumption of literature never dampened his onstage persona, which sometimes violent. Wardner vanished 25 years ago for reasons that have still not been explained. Although the length of his absence rendered him dead in the eyes of the law, his family always maintained that he would not kill himself. The fans have more elaborate theories, including that a botched suicide attempt left the singer permanently disfigured, and therefore reluctant to return. Rumours have persisted that Wardner murdered a young fan, before fleeing to escape justice, even though no solid evidence has been found to back up the claim. Wardner was recently confirmed as alive by his former band mates. There are even whispers he is preparing to record again.

Bonny Crawford seems to manage the band's 'estate', and given what she might know about the fate of that young fan she's remained tight-lipped. She steered the band out of the Manchester wilderness and onto a major label, where they gained the devotion of a recession-hit generation. In the process Crawford almost became a celebrity herself. Her ever-present fake fur coat and glossy heavy fringe was a look much imitated by female fans of the pop group.

Next month Crawford is unveiling an exhibition of paintings about Wardner. According to the press release, the pictures offer a loose chronology. Later pictures offer cryptic clues as to how he vanished, and promise to answer the unsolved mystery of why he did. At the time of going to press only a couple of previews of her pictures have been released. They suggest Crawford may have been hiding the light of her true talent under a bushel. Crawford has been evasive about how much she knows regarding Wardner's years 'off-grid' and what these pictures might reveal. She's clearly lost none of her ability to court publicity ahead of the exhibition. But whether or not there is a whiff of immorality about this remains to be seen.

Regardless, for too long Wardner has been remembered for his more bizarre behaviour and his disappearing act. This exhibition should put the focus back on his life and the brilliance of his music.

Sam phoned the gallery where her pictures were being exhibited. To his surprise, they passed on Bonny's telephone number. He rang it instantly, and after seven or eight rings a distant voice answered the phone. 'Bonny Crawford,' she said.

'Hello Miss Crawford, my name's Sam Forbes. I'm writing a

book about Robert Wardner.'

'What sort of a book?'

'I was a huge fan of the band. I wrote some of the early articles about them.'

Bonny exhaled. Clearly, someone had been hounding her who wasn't interested in the music.

Once in London, Sam took the tube west. He bounded up the escalator, his head spinning with what Bonny might disclose. He resolved that his first question would regard whether Robert owned a white transit van.

Sam found himself amongst louche, expansive streets with high windows. Notting Hill had a refined, aspirational air. The market was in full swing, and the snatches of Indian fragrances wafting through the air enchanted Sam as he looked for Cavendish Street. Bonny was waiting at the end of it.

Her once severe bob had now loosened, falling in waves as she sleeked it over her head. She picked Sam out through the crowd with a theatrical wave of her hand. As Sam approached she looked to him more like a sophisticated French actress than a manager of a post-punk band.

'Sam?'

'Thank you for agreeing to meet me.'

'It didn't sound like the usual hack piece.'

'I'm guessing not all of the people that call you want to talk about his music?'

She smiled.

'What is it?'

'You have no idea what you're getting into. I'm the edge of the rabbit hole, Sam.'

Bonny led Sam through the streets. The two of them weaved in and out of stalls selling caramelized peanuts and paella. 'Up here,' she said, throwing the sash around her neck and leading him up a steel staircase, attached to the side of a townhouse. The staircase connected to a low-ceilinged attic room, its large windows projecting over the bustling street fare.

'Let me show you my work,' she said.

Bonny's heels rang out across the wooden floor as she moved to the window, where a series of pictures were propped up on a semi-circle of easels. He could imagine her spending days in here, he thought. Lost in the past.

Sam could see various depictions of Wardner. Just as he was beginning to inspect them, Bonny pulled a high stool in front of Sam and propped herself up on it. She gestured for Sam to sit on a stool opposite.

'I'm keen to have a good look at those paintings,' he began.

'In a minute,' she answered. 'First I'd like to hear what you're doing with this book.'

'I think it's time someone told Robert's real story. I want to find him is because I want to hear why he vanished, straight from the horse's mouth.'

'So I'm guessing you don't believe the rumours?'

'I didn't. But yesterday a man tried to drive me in front of a ten tonne truck. It might have been my imagination, but...'

'You thought it was Wardner?'

Sam nodded. Bonny curled a lock of hair behind her ear. 'He has a tendency to appear in places that you least expect him. I don't mean literally. But a man can't vanish like that and not...haunt you somehow.' She turned to look at her pictures.

'I agree. But I find it very difficult to think he could have killed anyone. His songs had a lot of empathy.'

'Yes, but he wasn't all good, Sam. He certainly left a mark on my life, and not for the better.'

'Is that why you made these pictures?'

'See for yourself.'

Sam stood up and moved over to Bonny's pictures. At first he mistook the paintings for photographs, given the very skilful rendering.

One picture showed Wardner tugging on a cigarette, stood in front of what appeared to be a harbour.

'So is this about how he vanished?'

'Indeed.'

'Oh my god.'

As Sam stepped closer he saw that the paint used to depict the sea was in fact subtly composed of words. Shaped to reflect the contours of the ocean.

Inspecting, he gradually picked out phrases from National Grid songs. Wardner's body was framed with the phrase '*I can only find disorder*,' which Sam recognised from 'We Strive For Symmetry'. Amongst the ocean, he picked out the phrase '*Anything to escape the artificial light*' from 'A World Of Neon'.

'Know much about art, Sam?'

'Not really. That's more my girlfriend's forte.'

'She paints?'

'No, she curates at a gallery near us. They're having that Gavin Holding up soon and she won't stop going on about it. So what should this picture be telling me?'

'Well, this is my portrayal of the moment he vanished. Before he caught a ferry to Europe.'

'I thought that was only a rumour?'

Bonny's reaction was non-committal.

Sam stepped back, his mind racing. 'I can't help but wonder if you know where he is, but are saving that for the exhibition?'

'They're pieces of art, Sam.'

'What's this one about then?' he asked.

Taking pride of place in the window was a large painting of the band's album cover. Set against a corporate shade of rich green was a triangle split into six parts. Inside each segment, as on the album cover, was a word from the record's title, '*How I Left The National Grid*'. Except, where the album had used a glossy style of graphic design, Bonny had used thick brush strokes to achieve that effect. In her new guise she had clearly tapped into some nascent skill. On closer inspection, Sam could see more phrases subtly etched into the colour around the triangle.

'Is the choice of lyrics particularly meaningful?' he asked. At the bottom of the painting, he pointed at the phrase '*The wrong kind of divorce is murder*'.

'Of course,' she said, following his eyes. 'Ah, you noticed that one.'

'So does that tell us something about you and Wardner?'

He struggled to meet the intensity of her gaze.

'It tells you something about what he did to me,' she said.

Sam's mouth hung open. He couldn't think what to say.

'He's already rumoured to have murdered one woman. I can't help wondering...if you know something, aren't you morally obliged to say?'

'It's not for me to tell the world what Robert did,' she said. There was a strain on her face that suddenly shocked Sam. Even as Bonny's eyes moistened, something told him to be careful not to be taken in by any crocodile tears.

Yet, looking at Bonny as she walked into the bright light, Sam had a sense that something had happened which had left Bonny truly traumatised. Despite himself, he couldn't help feeling a little relieved when she turned and said. 'I'm sorry, Sam, but I think that is enough for today.'

ROBERT WARDNER

'This song is off our album,' I said, feedback piercing through the crowd. A twitching mass of misfits and freaks, straining to see through dry ice and lights. Every waif and stray you'd ever ignored, waiting for the revolution cry. I could just see them out there, jostling each other for a view of the stage. Black eyes and bruised ribs.

'It's out next week. But don't buy it.'

The crowd roared. Bonny, somewhere in the audience, pushed two small fists in the air. I could see her diamond ring glisten off the stage lights.

'The record company rushed it out because all they care about is M.O.N.E.Y.'

Theo grabbed his mike. 'But buy our record instead of anyone else's. Because no one else is capable of writing songs like this.'

Some cheered. As if encouraging an illegal boxing match between us. Wanting blood.

Theo turned to Jack and nodded for him to start playing 'Whitewashed'.

Jack looked at me, apologetic, counted us in. Began drumming. As Theo bent over to push his bass pedal I stuck two fingers up behind his back.

The crowd went mental.

There was a bed of snakes beneath us, coiling round each other and the music. Theo stood up, guessing what I'd done. Makeup running down his face.

I watched his lips move, cursing me.

I looked straight back at him. 'Do your fucking job,' I shouted.

The crowd were trying to push through the barrier.

The music was so loud we were been getting nosebleeds between each song. The minute an instrument was left alone it would scream out, like it was being neglected. We'd try and stem the blood with towels roadies left on the amps. Still crisp from the night before.

Theo looked down, trying to find his way into the song.

It's a song you have to throw yourself into. Jack's drums struggle to stay on top of this serrated guitar line Simon makes, by pulling the jack out of his guitar. Using the static tip of it to hammer discordant noise.

The riff went with this beat you use your body for. Theo's bassline sitting high on the song. Driving it to the chorus.

Except now he couldn't do that. The throb we had come to expect throughout the song wasn't there. He'd replaced it with a hard, three-note riff he was hammering out. Off-time. Throwing us all.

Deliberately.

In this song I had to shout lyrics in time to him. By nodding us in, and changing his part he knew I'd be lost.

'What are you doing?' I shouted.

Jack, looking between us. Trying to hold it down.

The audience wondering what the hell we were doing to the song.

Simon knew it was about to fall apart. It's the worst thing in the world, disintegrating in public like that. There was a TV crew too, cameras focusing every time I stood still.

Simon stood at the tip of the stage, black t-shirt clinging to his body. Hands reaching out, almost touching him. By that point of the tour he was unravelling. He'd watched Taxi Driver *one too many times the night before and shaved his hair into a Travis Bickle Mohican. He pulled out the jack for one scintillating riff, until the audience roared their recognition and then, shooting a look at Theo, he pulled close to me and stamped on his pedal.*

Started mimicking Theo's original part.

Pushing Theo out of the song.

I had seconds to find my way in. Closing my eyes, trying to get on top of that rhythm. Any minute now, I had to dictate it.

'They say it's progress,' *I started, feeling my voice fill the room,* 'I call it rejection. They say it's happiness. I call it dejection.'

This beloved hymn. The crowd chanting the song up at us.

'They say we can never go back, that the door is closed.'

I opened my eyes. Theo crouched over his bass. Simon was so close to me I could now smell the blood under his nose.

'But I don't think they can close it now.'

The song sped up, pushing to the chorus. Way ahead of time, Theo churning through the chorus riff.

I lost the moment to come in. Balled my fists, screamed at the ceiling.

Simon wheeled round to Theo. Nodding at him, coaxing him back into the song. Licking the blood that collected at the corner of his mouth. Specks of it, I saw, were on Theo's cheek.

Theo stood at the foot of the stage. Burning the bass riff for the outro.

In his own world.

Simon pushed a pedal and went closer to him, stood at his side. Until the fretboards of their guitars seemed like they could touch at any moment. Like a pilot guiding another down to the runway.

We were improvising, in front of thousands of people.

Off the map.

Jack sped up, trying to smother the confusion with skill.

The crowd baying. Us, moments from collapsing in full view.

'Find the chorus,' *Simon was shouting, to us all.* 'Twice round and then into the chorus. Got it?'

'You are fucking dead,' *I shouted at Theo.*

'Got it,' *he shouted back, Jack nodding.*

I grabbed the mike, shouting the words to the chorus. The crowd surged forward in one tidal wave, joining in. Simon and Theo threw their heads back.

'Stick with the song, for Christ's sake,' *Simon shouted.*

I was welded to the microphone. It was my turn to take charge. My fingers crackling down the stand, my lips braced to be stung by static off the mike.

It was a living nightmare.

It made me feel alive.

I closed my eyes, guided us to the outro. Not daring to look at Theo, praying for his sake he would keep playing along. Feeling the slow blaze of the guitar line, waiting for the section I ended and the three of them turned to one another for the climax.

When it came, Simon wheeled away from us all. A spinning, buzzing sound emanating from his guitar. His fingers shimmying up and down the fretboard, wrenching notes from it. Theo locking the groove down. Jack pummelling over the top.

I felt like I could flex my muscles and burst the walls with anger. Then something went off in me. A light bulb bursting.

I went over to the mike stand. A massive, black, metal thing. Nailed, with one loose bolt, to the stage.

I tore it out.

Theo watched me, stepping back, losing his grip on the bass. Simon let his notes fade early.

I wheeled it over my head.

Jack pummelled the cymbals.

I got some strength behind it and carved it round, over to Theo.

Let it go.

Theo dropped his bass and jumped into the crowd.

I watched it soar, like a strip of seaweed, the base of it dipping nobly into Theo's amp.

Tore right into it.

Sat in it.

Theo clambered back onstage, over to his bass. Raised it above his head and then, in time to Jack's cymbal wreckage, smashed it into the stage.

I hated the man but I had to give it to him.

Simon stood over his pedal, squeezing the last drops of life out of his guitar. Then snapped it silent, and took his guitar off.

Calm as you like. Professional.

Went to the back of the stage and placed it in its rack.

To the final, dying notes, I took a run up and threw myself into the crowd. I was just surfacing, to the sweat-drenched hair and ecstatic faces, when I heard smashing glass.

The crowd hoisted me up on their hands. Onstage I could see Theo.

Smashing every one of the lights at the front of the stage.
    One by one.
    I closed my eyes.
    Let them carry me.

5

Pouring her coffee, Elsa was startled by the snap of the letterbox.

Amongst the sheaf of paper-based noise was a brown envelope. It was addressed to Sam. She couldn't resist tearing it open.

Inside was a small white postcard. On it, in sloping, letters:

Call off your hunt right now, Sam. No one wants to be run into the ground. Not Wardner, not you. And certainly not your loved ones.

The final sentence made her eyes widen. She looked up the stairs, for evidence of movement, but there was none. The note was unsigned. She re-read it a few times, before looking for the postage stamp.

The letter had been posted in London.

Sam was struck by how drawn Elsa looked when he lolloped into the kitchen. The note was propped on the table against a vase. 'You didn't wake me,' he said.

She looked at the note. 'For you.'

'You opened my post?'

Sam scratched at his thin glaze of stubble and inspected it. 'Jesus.' He said. 'That's got my day off to a lovely start.'

Elsa closed her eyes, and Sam got the sense that she had carefully prepared her next comment. The pace, the tone, the smoothness. 'You promised , on the way home from our meal, that if Wardner started to go after you then you would call this off.'

'Call it off? I've got the commission. This is probably just some nutter fan. How could Wardner possibly know already about the book?'

The image of the man in the white transit van flashed across his mind. Sam decided to supress it. Bonny was right, he thought. It could have been anyone. Elsa nodded, slowly.

'Oh, come on,' Sam said. 'Don't be like that.'

'No.' she snapped. 'You're not doing this today. I only have a few hours left to get everything right for the exhibition. I'm not going to blow my one chance to prove myself to Malcolm because of your pig-headedness.'

'Pig-headedness? Well, a good morning to you, Sam,' he answered, closing his eyes.

Elsa grabbed her purse. 'It mentioned your loved ones,' she hissed. 'You know what that means? That means me.'

Elsa slammed the door, leaving in her wake a cold atmosphere for his guilt to fester in. Sam ran up to the bedroom, pushing his slim, silver laptop onto the bed.

He kept thinking how easily the explanation of a 'nutter fan' had come to him. It was almost as if he had been ready for this threat. What was it about the band's followers that made him think this wouldn't be beyond them? With the move, Sam hadn't been able to visit the fans' forum for a while. Had word of the book spread to them yet?

Having logged in on the sparsely designed, white and blue site he saw a number of new threads. The titles 'ROBERT WARDNER, ALIVE AND WELL' and 'ROBERT EXHIBITION' jumped out. But the top one, with 165 messages, was titled 'NEW ROBERT BOOK DUE'. It stretched to five pages.

Sam clicked to open it, found the start of the thread. He did not recognize the profile name of 'Shrinkingviolet'. It came with a picture of a dark-eyed girl in a leopard print scarf, an image small enough to resist proper scrutiny of her persona. She had written:

There's a new Robert book coming out next year. Apparently it intends to 'finally tell Robert's story' by interviewing those closest to him, and 'the man itself'. It's written by Sam Forbes, who covered the band's early years.

It then linked to a page on Mason House's website where, under 'Forthcoming Titles', there was a blurb of the book with an out of date photo of Sam, his hair long and almost matted. He clicked quickly back to see the replies.

> Not sure how it can hear from 'the man himself' when we only found out he was even alive a few weeks ago. Unless this Forbes is going to be shoving a microphone in a sick man's face while he tries to recover.

The next commenter had a profile picture of The Joker from *Batman*. He had written:

> Doesn't say Robert's consented to be interviewed. I'm guessing the author will be less bothered about making sure Robert returns fit and well, and more bothered about $. Scum.

The first reply to that entry had come from a user called 'darkcloud'. His temperament and fascinating outlook concisely illustrated by the chosen icon of a balled fist, blood curling between the knuckles:

> This arsehole is going to try and prove Wardner was a killer. We all know he wasn't, but Forbes will probably hassle the guy 'til he cracks, then write a book about what a psycho he is. These hacks are fucked up! He won't care if Wardner ends up dead, or behind bars. When Exit Discs were giving Simon a hard time Wardner smashed up the car of the head exec, while he was in it. Why don't we scare this sicko off for good too?

Sam stopped himself from reading the rest of the comments. Not until my home life is under control, he thought. He closed the page.

ROBERT WARDNER

Bonny pushed me into Cunningham's cramped office. Letters and press reports spilling off every surface. Bank statements.

'So you're not going to try and kill me today?' Cunningham asked, slouched in his chair.

He never looked at you. Not when he was talking to you, not when he was talking about you.

'Robert wants us to get this sorted,' Bonny said.

Cunningham looked at the grocer, who scribbled. They're always writing, lawyers, but you never get to see any of it.

'You've not brought your mate along this time then?' Cunningham said, brushing his shoe with a hand.

'He doesn't want this to get legal,' Bonny said.

'Is your baby too spoilt to speak for himself? Old enough to drive his car into mine, but not to deal with the consequences?'

'He's not a baby, and I'm not his babysitter. If anyone should be keeping a protective eye on him it's you. He entrusted his work to you. You're exploiting it.'

Cunningham shrugged. Looked at me.

'Nothing?'

'Believe me, it's better that I speak for him. He's taken down bigger men than you.' She looked to the generous bulge at his waistline. 'Believe it or not.'

He narrowed his eyes.

'You're just starting in this business, Bonny. Do you really want to go down with this ship? There'll be an unpleasant smell around you that won't go away if you do. If you fight me, I'll make sure you never manage another band again. There won't be a spotty four-piece in the world that'll go near you. I'll make you that toxic.'

'This isn't about me, Andrew. It's about them. You were pretty unreasonable during the meeting. You were forcing them to promote an album that they say isn't ready, reneging on all the reasons the band

signed with you. Not exactly the front you presented when you courted them, is it?'

'I had no idea they were going to churn through producers like they're sweets in a hotel lobby.'

'You signed up for the journey. This is their livelihood. Robert will pay for the damage to your car…'

'Bon?'

She waved a hand at me, 'And allow the album to come out too, if you don't sue him.'

Cunningham smiled.

Had me where he wanted me.

'If he wants to battle…' I started.

'What?' Cunningham said, leaning forward. 'You really want to battle? Your album will recoup the money we laid out for you, and our lawsuit will make sure you're too busy gripping the oak to ever record again. You're finished either way.'

'Why are you doing this?' Bonny said. 'You got into a business working with artists, but at the first sign of trouble you screw them over.'

'Don't buy into it, Bon,' I said. 'He wants me to lose it. Then they can add that to their list of grievances and use that as well. They're vultures.'

Bonny's hand went on my shoulder. 'What do you want to do then, Rob?' She started whispering. 'You have little option.'

Cunningham leaned forward. 'She's right, sport. You have no choices. The record comes out next month. And as well as fixing the car with your money, I want it valeted and cleaned too. By you, personally.'

'And then you won't sue?' I had to admire how Bonny kept fighting.

The grocer laid down his pen. Cunningham looked straight at Bonny. 'Oh, he said. 'Let's not make promises we can't keep.'

I lunged for him then. A thin arm, wrapped in fur, holding me back. He chuckled.

'You don't scare me,' he said.

6

Perhaps it was the sheer number of people within it, but the gallery in which Elsa worked seemed larger than Sam remembered. Walls that were bare only a few hours ago were now resplendent with Gavin Holding's lavish cityscapes.

Sam took a glass of champagne from a side table and made his way over to a piece. Elsa was nowhere to be seen. A man with a monocle told Sam to fetch him an orange juice, which only exacerbated his feeling that he should be serving the champagne, not drinking it.

Each picture portrayed a different modern landscape. 'Mezzanine' depicted a clean white cube of a home. The surrounding grass had started to reclaim it.

Sam pretended to deeply consider the pictures on the wall as he sensed Elsa's eyes at the back end of the room. But her gaze eluded him. He learnt that her eye movements were in fact intended for her boss Malcolm, stood just a few feet away behind him. Embarrassed by his efforts he recoiled, wondering if he had ever seen her in that tight, revealing red dress before. It accentuated curves of her body, ones that her outfits rarely flaunted. A man with half-moon glasses was looking down at a cheque book and her cleavage at the same time. Elsa was motioning to Malcolm.

Sam had never seen Elsa so invigorated, her skin rosy and her muscles clenched.

As he finished his glass he realized how dense the air was, clouded by all the gassy exchanges. He needed to take a breath.

He had his head down as he approached the door. It was only as the breeze from the outside pushed onto him that he realized Bonny was standing in the doorway.

The fur on her coat bristled in the wind and the glittered shadow around her eyes was darker, giving her a glamorous, gothic air.

'Well, I didn't expect to see you here,' she said.

Somehow, he didn't believe her.

Her manner had changed, from the bruised brusqueness of her farewell into something more provocative.

Sam faltered for a moment. 'My girlfriend organised the exhibition. Didn't I mention it?'

'Oh yes,' she said. 'And what a fine job she's done.'

Bonny turned to the older man who she'd entered with, one with the arched eyebrow and air of long-endured suffering one might expect from a restaurant critic. 'Excuse me a moment,' she said, 'Sam is just going to give me a tour of the gallery.'

'What brings you this far north then?' he asked, easing his way through the bodies.

'Well, trips like this are all part of my new career, Sam,' she said. 'Holding has been quite an inspiration to me. I had to see his work in person.'

'Really?'

'You don't like his pictures? Don't you think they are similar to mine at all?'

They both contain messages, Sam thought. But his are for everyone, and yours are just to Wardner.

'I don't know,' he answered.

He felt conscious of eyes upon him. He looked up to see Elsa, the icy expression that he had long associated with her now very apparent.

'I'm glad we bumped into one another, Sam. I've been feeling guilty. I think I must have freaked you out the other day.'

'I can handle it,' Sam said, meeting Elsa's eye.

'She doesn't look very happy with you,' Bonny said.

It occurred to him that in her coat Bonny tonight resembled a caricature of the persona that had almost made her famous.

'Excuse me a moment.'

He moved towards Elsa.

'You've done a great job. I can't believe how many people are here,' he began.

'So you thought you'd invite your childhood crush to the opening night?' she hissed, her voice low enough to be submerged in the surrounding babble. Her shop front smile remained intact.

'Not at all. She's an artist now. She's come to check out your show. She's a huge fan of Holding's.'

Elsa's raking gaze took in the fur coat in one sweep. 'She's aged badly,' she whispered, passing a flute of champagne to a passing guest.

'That's a bit harsh.'

'That's what that line of work will do to you.'

'What line of work?'

'Chasing after madmen.'

At that moment Malcolm arched backwards, gesturing wildly with his hands for the benefit of two buyers. He knocked over two glasses of champagne in the process, throwing foam over the walls.

'Which you never do,' Sam answered, nodding at her boss.

'I have to get on, Sam. Here, take your lady friend a glass of bubbly. She'll love that.'

Turning back he was surprised to see Bonny was already at his side.

'Something has just occurred to me, Sam. Would you be interested in meeting Theo?'

She received the flute with her fingertips.

'Well, yes,' he said, torn between the question and the penetrating stare that Elsa had again kindly just made available.

She sipped. 'Because I have an exhibition of my work soon, and we thought it would be fun to combine it with a performance of National Grid songs.'

'With Wardner singing?'

'You'll have to wait and see.'

Sam drank. 'So why are you doing this for me?'

'I don't want my anxiety about Wardner to be the only account on record.'

'You don't strike me as the anxious type.'

'Well to be honest, I felt bad about the impression I gave you.' There was mischief in her eyes. For a moment Sam could see the iconoclastic manager from days past.

'It's in London I presume.'

'What's in London?' Elsa asked, handing Sam a fresh glass of champagne out of nowhere.

Sam looked between his girlfriend and Bonny.

'The future of art. And, an exhibition of my work about Wardner,' Bonny said. 'Which might warrant an appearance from the man himself.'

Elsa looked penetratingly at Sam, who shrugged. Sam had the sense that the quiet exchange somehow satisfied Bonny.

A few minutes later Sam was finishing the glass as the gallery began to quieten.

'You're not leaving the exhibition now?' Elsa asked, moving up to him. 'Before the after-party?'

'Bonny offered to answer a few more questions about Wardner, if I took her for a drink.'

'I need you here, Sam. I can't get through this on my own.'

'But I can't miss this opportunity.'

'You're still doing this, despite what I think. If you go into her trap, you're making a choice to completely ignore me, Sam,' she said. 'You don't think she has ulterior motives?'

'I doubt she's trying to get me into bed!'

Just at that moment Bonny laughed in the distance. It was the joyous sound of someone thoroughly in control.

'You know she works for him. That he'll have her wrapped around her finger.'

'It's just a chat.'

She fixed her eyes on Sam for a moment, and Sam sipped. Sensing the impasse, she blew her hair off her face, and sighed. 'I have to get on,' she said, shaking her head as she moved away.

The cut of her dress, and the way it held her body transfixed him as she departed. I should have told her that, he thought.

Elsa was engaged in an effusive conversation with Holding when Sam returned, a hurriedly filled rucksack lopped over his shoulder. Sam felt sure that when he did leave with Bonny, Elsa didn't even notice.

Elsa had been following his movements with the corners of her eyes, and her glassy smile dropped the moment she saw Sam slip out.

'Is everything alright, my dear?' Malcolm asked, placing his hand on her shoulder.

The cold breeze from the outside world chilled her shoulders. Malcolm's aftershave offered an unexpected balm.

'It was a triumph,' Malcolm said, his aloofness lessened by the exchange of money. His hands seemed keen to go anywhere.

She was surprised by his proximity, but the combination of wine and relief left her open to it. Malcolm somehow appeared ten years younger.

'You really thought so? I was worried that the Qatar set wouldn't sell.'

'Oh yes, that one requires a really dedicated lover of art.'

Malcolm leaned in.

'It was your powers of persuasion that sold it, Elsa.'

To her surprise, she found herself able to absorb the remark. Despite her tight evening dress she no longer felt self-conscious, but empowered. Sam was gone. The evening had suddenly opened, like an orchid.

'I'll always be grateful for the shot you gave me tonight, Malcolm,' she said.

'All this,' Malcolm said, gesturing around him, 'can wait until tomorrow. I have a rather bracing bottle of Moët at my house, which I have been saving for an occasion just as this. Would you care to join me?'

Elsa didn't answer. But she felt surprised by the lack of revulsion within her as she allowed herself to be led towards his car.

ROBERT WARDNER

When I went missing, people thought I must have planned it all out. But it doesn't work like that.

It was a game I'd been playing with myself, as things got worse. Whenever Bonny gave me cash for something, I put it in a locked box under my bed. If I got hold of an item of clothing people had never seen me wear, I put it in there too.

I'll never do it, I told myself.

Then one night, three months after they put the album out, something snapped. That morning I'd got a letter from Cunningham saying he was suing me, for the expenses of re-recording the album.

Just two days ago he had said he would reconsider it.

How cowardly is that, to give you false hope?

I went for a quiet drink off Oldham Street, with Simon and Nicola. The War Committee. No Frankie. Despite what she'd promised in her wedding vows, she made herself scarce when it got difficult.

In the pub there was the same bloke in the grey mac. He was sitting at the jukebox, by himself when I walked in. As I waited for the bar man he called out to me. 'Out for a quiet pint?' he shouted. I turned and faced him. 'Here's to some alone time!' he roared.

I gritted my teeth, looked at the optics. Kept gritting them. Until Simon arrived.

Soon he came, flapping his hands against his coat. Nicola behind him, looking as if she'd pulled out her curlers at the last minute. 'What's wrong?' he said. 'You look like you've seen a ghost.'

'The bloke by the jukebox,' I said. 'He's been following me.'

Simon turned. 'There is no bloke at the jukebox. What are you drinking?'

'Guinness.'

He waved a crumpled fiver at the barmaid. She had on velvet gloves up to her elbows.

'Must be tricky washing the pint glasses with those gloves.' She smiled. 'I miss the old jukebox,' he said. 'No one gives a shit about these new haircut bands.'

I could leave all this behind, I thought.

'I've got to play you The Cure's last record, Rob. They're starting to do it. Make soundscapes with keyboards. All the things we've talked about.'

'We never found an end-point when we did that. Soundscapes, keyboard drones. We'll end up like Yes. You remember The Smiths at The Hacienda? That's the future. Building a connection, one-by-one, with every member of the audience. Being a different band for each one of them.'

'I can't see you with gladioli down your trousers, Rob.'

'I've got bigger fish to fry at the moment, mate.'

'Cunningham won't really sue you,' Simon said, his Guinness settling. 'Think about it, Rob, how the hell would that work? They paid you an advance, agreed to fund you making the record, then went back on it and forced one out. How can he sue you for that? He's just pissed off about the car.'

'At least I got to him,' I said.

'You got to him too much though. His car was his pride and joy. So now he's thinking, what's Robert's? His music. But he's chucking about threats he can't back up.'

'What do we know about solicitors though? We're just a couple of dickheads with synthesisers. I can't fight him by myself.'

Nicola looked at Simon, nodded encouragingly. 'What?' Simon said. 'Tell him.'

Simon looked at me, hands deep in pockets. 'We'll stick with you, mate. We've got a bit saved. We'll use it to fight them.'

'Why would you do that?'

Nicola crossed her legs. Sequins, dimly sparkling under the bar lights.

'Well what options have this lot got without you, Rob? Theo will end up as a male hairdresser. Or worse, a full-time DJ. We didn't form your band because we had too many options.'

'You wouldn't know it, from how Theo and Jack are carrying on,' I said.

'They're not really quitting the band,' Simon said. 'They just said that because of that stuff with Cunningham's car. Personally, I'm glad you smashed his shit motor. It's proper rock star behaviour, that. We'll make another record.'

'But the album, Si. We put years into it. It could have really been good.'

Touched a nerve there.

'Well, what can I say, Rob?'

'You thought Vicente cracked it, didn't you? You thought it was done?'

'Let's not get into it. Let's get smashed.'

'Nah. Not tonight.'

After that, Simon would barely leave my side. I must have looked a right mess.

'Where's Frankie?' Nicola asked. 'I was hoping we would get to catch up.'

'Don't want to talk about it.'

'You had a falling out?'

'Worse.'

I forced myself to stay in their company. However much I drank, my thinking was that if I was with others then it wasn't too bad. Nicola kept saying 'Are you alright?' and I'd nod, but the light had gone out. When the two of them left me alone at the bar I felt crushed. No Frankie, no band, no money, no future.

I remember looking at the glass, forgetting how to drink from it. How many gulps you took in one go. How to even hold it.

Simon and Nicola walked part of the way home with me, and at the end of my street watched me move into the horizon.

I remember as I took the last few steps, I had this funny feeling. I could imagine Simon looking at the back of my head and taking in details he never had before. About how I walked, what I wore.

Saving what I looked like, trying to hold onto it.

That was the moment all the ambitions of our youth were left behind. I could imagine Nicola pulling him back home, telling him I'd be fine.

At that moment our world was being silently torn open. In the twenty five years that followed the tear got bigger, letting in everything dark and twisted the universe had to offer.

I was a few paces from my door when I turned and saw the man in the grey mac stood there. Smoking.

Now he knew where I lived.

I ran the rest of the way.

When I got inside, there was a court summons waiting for me.

That was when I decided. I had to get out of there. Leave a gap where I once was.

I had the place to myself. I had a bit of room to work out what to do.

I pulled the box out from under the bed, put on the clothes in it and stashed the notes in my pockets. Went to the pub next door, ordered a taxi from outside a house a few streets away. It was November, and winter had muscled in quickly. It was starting to get icy cold, but that just made me act faster. I had to make it look as if perhaps I hadn't made it home so I didn't take photos, toothbrushes, food. Just those few things people didn't know I owned. And Nataly's phone number, on that receipt.

Kept my hood up in the taxi. 'Bit late to be going to the station, isn't it?'

They always want to know your story, taxi drivers. It helps them to carry on being right about everything.

'Got an early morning meeting,' I said.

'Meeting?'

I could see him look me over in the mirror.

In that state of mind, you don't want people asking you questions. You try and mind your own business and everyone wants to know what you had for breakfast. But when you're crying out for someone to turn to, no one wants to know.

All the way there I fingered the receipt.

At Piccadilly I called the number. 'Nataly,' I said. 'It's me.'

She sounded unbelievably tired. I pictured her scribbling away in her room. 'Robert? How you doing, you alright?'

'I'm coming to London.'

'Tomorrow night?'

'Tonight.'

'Everything alright with you and Francesca?'

I watched the football crowd spill out the pub opposite. They threw their arms around each other and cheered. 'She doesn't know I'm coming.'

Nataly sighed.

'I don't want to get involved, Robert.'

'No one knows I'm coming to you. And you won't tell anyone. Will you, Nataly?'

What if Nataly said that in fact she would, I thought. What if she said, don't do this, Rob. I don't want to say it, but go back to your wife. Go back to your career. It's not too bad, you've got a record in the shops. They paid you some money, a decent deal for people new on the scene. People round town know your face. You've made something out of this ridiculous circus. Don't blow it.

What would happen if you were at your lowest ebb, and the person you'd decided would be there told you to forget it?

It's the river for you, if that happens.

'No, I won't,' she said, quietly.

'Good. Because I've got nowhere else to go. You're not going to let me down, are you?'

'Don't worry, Robert, I'm here.'

'That had better be true. Is there someone there?'

'No. There's no one here. When are you getting in?'

I wouldn't see Frankie again. I wouldn't get to be the husband she deserved. Build a life as a normal man. I wouldn't press my body against her any more.

'I don't know. Can we meet tomorrow morning?'

'Course. I'm working from eleven. But I can get you set up before then. I'll be home again for you in the evening.'

Silence.

'The train's here.'

I had until tomorrow to get as far as I could. By midday, Bonny would be making calls. My parents. Simon, Nicola. Why did you let him drink, if he was like that?

It was a quiet pint, Simon would say.

Well, where is he? She'd ask around.

Nataly's number wouldn't be on her list.

I got on the train, found a quiet carriage, with only a couple of men in oil rig uniforms, dozing.

The reflection in the window gave an uncensored version of myself. I was unable to meet my eye, ashamed of what it would give off.

Thought about what I was going to do when I got to London.

Whether Nataly could really offer me a way out.

I only managed a couple of hours' kip. I felt a bit better for every minute I travelled, knowing I was inching further away. I looked out at cold, grey England and thought about the life I'd left, in some corner of the North.

I thought of the days spent kicking footballs against walls, waiting for my Mum to warn me Dad was on his way home. I thought of desolate teenage wastelands, played out in cubicles and against sinks. I thought of Simon and me clambering up rubble, looking for the future on building sites. Dancing in nightclubs, skirting portals that looked into the meaning of the city. The first time I showed Simon some lyrics in his bedroom. The first cigarette Frankie and I shared, tucking the stub from the pictures inside my sock after. Just knowing. I thought of when I proposed to her, as we shared a bag of chips and watched the cranes rebuild our city. The sparkle in her eyes as she said yes, before she hugged me.

I pressed my face against the sticky glass. Closed my eyes. Tried not to think about it all.

In London I found a hotel for the night, turfing thoughts out my mind with all my remaining energy. I had dreams about swimming in a dark channel, grey sludge pouring in my mouth. Woke up covered in sweat, feeling cornered. In the morning the past clamoured to get in with the winter sun.

In the early light the city looked brittle. I didn't find the glass buildings ugly. They were new surfaces I could find a new face in. The slate had been wiped clean.

I called Nataly. Agreed to meet her outside The British Library before her shift.

Started to wonder if I'd done the right thing. Without your friends, without your partner, the world is harsh.

I bought a coffee from a kiosk and sat on a concrete bollard in the square off Euston Road. Amongst that clear morning light it was like a sandblasted utopia. That square glowed with an almost religious quality. Sun rose over the skyscrapers, lighting the square gradually, making the buildings look internally ablaze. The glossy windows framed this fresh white light, and I felt as new as the edifices around me. They hid the ugly past of the city, and amongst this cleansing light I felt I had buried my past.

Outside the sombre café a bearded bloke in a hunting cap lingered by the bin. A policeman chased him along and he went, reluctantly. I knew there were hostels in Spitalfields and Whitechapel, for homeless men. Was that me, now?

I wondered if she would even come, or if I'd have to go home. Face up to it all.

At that moment, Nataly was the only person in my new life.

She was early, and walked towards me quickly. I was glad I hadn't rung when she was in a hole. She stood at a distance as she greeted me. Her hair longer now, shot through with a red strand.

'What is going on?' she said. Something twitching in her eyes.

'I know it's weird, turning up like this.'

She shook her head.

'I'm glad you thought of me.'

'Why?'

She wasn't having it. 'You look like you need a good meal, Robert.'

We walked to her flat. It wasn't far off Holborn. I didn't say much on the way there, just looked at the skeletal trees. It was like ancient London round there. Another world. Nataly lived in an upstairs apartment, overlooking this tree-lined square. Her parents had money, that much was obvious. Everything was beige, brown shutters on windows. Charcoal self-portraits everywhere. Her in her undies, or with veins popping out of her arms.

'Do you live alone?' I asked, as she boiled the kettle.

She pursed her lips. She'd wondered when it'd come up.

'My boyfriend's gone to Canada.'

'He still your boyfriend?'

'No. He's working there. Most of his stuff is out.'

She took our drinks into the living room. Canvases on the floor, most of them turned to the wall. A mannequin wrapped in her mum's chocolate-brown fur coat. Degas postcards, prints from Fellini films. That world she'd sketched out in her letters, laid out in front of me.

I could walk amongst it.

Frankie never had any of that, I thought. Just mild curiosity. But Nataly's got this whole world, pushed under the surface. Vibrant. Richer than mine.

I want to live in it, I thought. No one's given it the time of day and she keeps it in here, behind these shutters. It's not like mine. Tattered, badly thought out. Her world is clear, crystalline. It has its own landscape that only she knows. She'll make it.

If I don't stop her.

She had a funny look on her face. 'What is it?'

'I've just realized something. The landlord's left. His son has taken over since Mike's been away.'

'Mike is your boyfriend?'

'Ex.'

'So why are you smiling?'

She looked me square in the eyes. 'Because his son will think you're Mike, won't he?'

I looked at the records.

'Don't you see, Rob? That'll help with you trying to keep a low profile.'

I looked at the records. Low, The Scream, Faith. All perfectly preserved in aspic. Pillars in her world.

I could live here.

I took the drink. 'What makes you think I want to?' I asked.

She sat on the sofa. 'I've seen you in better states.'

She tucked her legs under herself. Muscular, caramel-coloured. 'You going to talk to me then, Robert? What's going on?'

I put the coffee down, watched it cool.

I'll ruin this place, I thought.

I stayed at Nataly's a few months longer than I should have done. She left me to my own devices in the day, and once I'd grown a bit of a beard I started walking round the frozen suburbs. I walked round and round them as if, bit by bit, I could tread off my problems. The suburbs seemed to have their own sense of loss, and I left something in them. I learnt them as if they were my own set of prayers. Walking eased the tension in my mind. Even in rain, sleet and snow I pressed my problems into the pavement and left them to hum down there.

I knew I'd lost weight, but I was still glad no one recognised me.

Gradually, this new Robert emerged from the ashes. In my mind I had got so battered that I'd eventually been forced out of one life and into another realm. That was what it felt like, Nataly's. Like this netherworld I'd slipped into, where my concerns couldn't reach me. The legal battle with Exit Discs, the problems with Frankie and the band, they were like night terrors that I'd managed to almost forget. I felt like going back to my previous life would be as stupid as attempting to relive a nightmare. Nataly gave me access to the bank account Mike had left, and I started drawing money out of it. With those few possessions Nataly was able to give me, I started again.

It is amazing how little you need to get by. How much one person's benediction can sustain you. After a few weeks Nataly stopped looking at me with fear in her eyes. She picked up on this new calm in me, and I sensed a plan coming together in her head. One windy afternoon, while the gusts shook the window frames in her kitchen, she brought out her acoustic guitar. When she offered it to me I held it like it was someone else's baby. While I ran my hands up and down it she showed me her notebooks, with these ideas for songs sketched out in them. 'A lot of this is unfinished,' she said, looking at them like a doctor with a prescription pad. In small italics, there were lyrics on one page, mirrored by details about production on the other.

She performed each, on the edge of her bed, in a husky voice, miles away from the commanding tone she'd had on stage. Occasionally pain would be writ on her face as she'd hint at some coda. In her stay-pressed white shirt, her hair pinned up, it was strange to see some office worker putting across such a vortex of emotion. It took me a while to realise what she was doing. She was giving me a banquet to feast on, by slowly encouraging me to step into my own imagination once again.

I could see why she had closed the blinds for so long. Even how she crashed from time to time. Her inner world was so strong, so detailed, I think she'd have felt it indecent to spend too long with the outside world, and all its dead alleys. These sketches that she then played to me were almost ready to be introduced to the world. At that moment in time she was a minor musician, but one who was gradually gaining more and more attention. The world knew of maybe five or six songs she had written, and I knew even they had taken years to write. But Nataly had so much more than that to hit them with. That afternoon I learnt that in her red spiral-bound notebooks whole albums were sketched out. Not one album she was pouring it all into, like me, but a whole sequence. She walked me through their brittle landscapes, hesitantly at first. She used female characters for her songs. Catherine De Barra and Becky Sharp were two of her favourite mouthpieces. Through them the anger she felt, at all the sexism, apathy and corruption, was expressed. These characters gave her, three verses at a time, new territories on which she could map the unspoken. One song in particular made my heart stop, showed me the real Nataly. 'White Tiles' expressed, in a few minor chords, this hidden bathroom culture she'd felt trapped in as a teenager. Self-harming to let out mental pressure whilst schoolgirls giggled in the toilet mirror. In another, 'The Gale Through The Trees', she recast herself as a widow, living in a spectral house on top of a hill. Drawing freezing water from a well every day and spending the nights praying for forgiveness. This was Nataly doing what only a true artist can. Seizing her phantoms, one by one, and trapping them in songs.

A new ritual emerged. As soon as she came back from work, before she'd eaten, she would come through the door and pick up her guitar. It was up to me to join her, sit and listen. To stop whatever odd activity I was caught up in, and be an audience. On the occasions I didn't, when my head was stuck somewhere, she'd stop after a few verses and it would be hard to get her to speak again.

I realized then that I was playing an essential role for her. One that she would probably die without. I was her inner audience. As she played, flat city light filtering through the blinds of her bedroom, I could imagine whole arrangements for these songs. I told her what I thought, in a low voice after the final note ended. She'd look up at me, excited and expectant, and I had to get my verdict right, otherwise her mouth would twist into disdain. But if I was accurate in my assessment she'd nod, or say 'Oh god, yes,' and make notes in the margins of her notebooks.

In the end there were four of them, lined up on the small shelf above her bed. Four albums. Her future legacy, stacked in a space that took up less room than an average tea-set. 'Those notebooks there,' I'd say. 'Will outlast anything I'll do.'

There's this misconception that artists should create their own mythologies, through how they live. Not true. They should create their own mythologies through their work. In whatever styles, textures and approaches they choose to use.

In return for this intimate tutorage Nataly shopped, cooked and fed me. She never asked why I couldn't do these tasks myself. She knew that if she didn't I'd grow thin, and waste away. Sometimes I thought she didn't want me to learn how. If I did, it would be the first step towards me leaving.

When night fell, we'd listen to records. Lying on the floor of her front room, under low lamp-light. Seeing how reverently she chose tracks made me remember why I had even wanted to be a musician. Not out of anger, or some weird need to be famous. But because I truly believed that these sounds created whole worlds that, unlike the world outside our window, endured. I remember watching Nataly, kneeling in paint-flecked shorts and a vest top, tugging this lock of hair from her eyes as she studied the sleeve to Kate Bush's Never Forever. One of her favourites was The Cure's 'Charlotte Sometimes' and at night I'd dream of her lilting voice, absently singing it as she cooked. We never talked about the unusual way we were communing with one another, through songs.

Other nights we'd drink a glass of red wine while The Cocteau Twins' Lullabies built a spider's web around us. The woody, scarlet world depicted in the cover art the same texture, in my mind, as Nataly's world. I realized that records were living spaces, and that if you allowed yourself to you could exist in their architecture. Even if they were cold and foreboding places, like mine. Full of twisted metal, and out-of-control machines.

One day, Nataly came home from work and gave me a blank notebook of my own. 'What's this for?' I asked.

'What do you think?' she said. 'Take your time.'

I only wrote one, slow, shifting song. Thumbing chord after chord, a few phrases leaking in. When I played it back to her, Nataly said, 'Oh, Robert. That's one of mine.' And she opened up her notebook, and showed me.

When that didn't work she tried this different approach. One day I came back from my walk to see a Nikon camera on my bed. This bulky one, I could imagine some journalist taking to Beirut.

That afternoon she finished work early, and insisted we walk around Spitalfield market while it was busy and vibrant. Nataly wore a red anorak, and as she browsed delicatessen stalls I took photos of this beguiling, dark-haired woman playing the character of a rich heiress, with her hands. She laughed and joked with the market traders, and when one juggled two cherries to make her laugh the sound reverberated *around me, like a beautiful ocean wave. The photos I took were of a new woman. Less a strained ballerina, and more a glamorous damsel from a murder mystery. Her tousled, dark hair sticking to her nylon dress, and a touch of colour reddening her lips. I saw then how I was shaping her too with my lens, in the moments I captured her. Styling her for a future that I was perhaps imagining. We were both at the age were such thoughts seemed important. When the world still felt like a playground. When we believed that what we did was significant, a debt paid to the future.*

There's this one picture of Nataly that I took that afternoon that I still take everywhere I go. We took it in a Victorian tearoom that she dragged me to.

In the shot she's standing next to a vase of roses at the counter. Behind her are plump cakes in glass domes. Nataly is looking just off-centre, smiling. Her hair has fallen over one eye and the other is smeared with glittering eye shadow. In this picture I can smell the fresh sponge cake, the rich scent of brewed coffee.

The Nataly depicted in it was never fully realized. She never completely embodied that mellow, satisfied Nataly, whose face portrayed thoughts about the future. When I look at that picture I think how I would do anything to will that Nataly into existence. I knew even then that one day I would trail around London, looking for traces of that afternoon. For a remnant, a hint, anything, that recalled the Nataly that fleeted in and out of reckoning that day. That afternoon a shard of an imagined future had fallen into our hands, and at that point we hadn't yet squeezed it so tight that it drew blood.

I told Nataly that one day I'd pay her back for everything, that it was all a loan. But she just said she needed me to stay with her. Said she needed me around for when her life grew dark, for next time she crashed. The rituals changed. Instead of playing records together, she'd lug her gramophone out onto the thin exile of her balcony, and close it behind her. Singing to herself as she smoked a Malboro Light, with her mum's brown fur coat wrapped around her shoulders. She'd gaze at a fixed point in the distance, blowing smoke carefully out at the blue horizon. Sometimes I wondered if she chose that spot because she knew it faced Canada.

Not long after that I started to want to move on. She was beginning to sculpt me into the boyfriend she no longer had. Got me wearing his coats. I felt myself getting sucked in. I had to get out.

I went to the nearest passport office. Introduced myself as 'Mike'. Told them I'd lost my passport, and they issued me with a temporary one.

7

The view of the city from the window was very different to the one Elsa was accustomed to. The houses outside reflected a gentler light than the sodium glare of the quayside. Elsa took a deep breath and made an effort to absorb the opulent feeling that emanated from the cool surfaces, shimmering off the piano, and the carefully mounted pictures.

'These are all the paintings I have felt unable to sell,' Malcolm said, moving over to the fridge. Elsa placed her coat around a black wicker chair.

'I remember us getting a few large offers for that one,' Elsa remarked, looking up at the glacial block of blue that commanded the central wall. 'You've kept that one to yourself.'

She took a sip of the offered wine, and felt a secret rhythm inside herself adjust. She was used to adopting a dismissive, flighty rhythm with Sam. But the distant city lights in the window, and the strong scent of the wine made her internally slow, to a more measured pace. She felt something bloom inside herself, and she hoped Malcolm would be sensitive enough to handle it.

Malcolm seemed concerned by a thought, but he then set his glass down and moved over to her. That scent grew stronger. 'Art like that will soon be a part of your life too,' he said, his voice lower. 'I have no doubt of it.'

Almost mocking the situation that was unfolding, Elsa raised her chin to him. With a small swallow, Malcolm took the tip of it between his thumb and forefinger and leant in. Elsa felt a sharp pang of guilt as he kissed her, both of their mouths remaining closed. Then, with an almost theatrical step, he moved even closer. His hand nested in her hair, and the kiss gradually gained intensity.

'It is far too late for you to get a taxi home,' he said.

'Yes,' Elsa replied, feeling suddenly very weak.

ROBERT WARDNER

I remember sitting in a café at the ferry terminal in Dover. Having a scalding cup of coffee and a limp sausage roll. The stain it made on the napkin as I watched the cars come off my ferry. Asking myself if I was really going to do this. Leave England. Taking in the weird lullabies of this land, that throbbed out of the fruit machines. Gulls circling outside the window, swooping on abandoned chips in the car park.

Sleepwalking onto the ferry.

Sitting on the upper deck in the stinging wind and thinking, it starts here. The realization hit me like a truck.

After that, Europe is almost a blank.

From what I can piece together I hitchhiked south from Calais. Must have got a lift from a lorry driver who took me as far as Lyon. I've got this distant memory of waking up soaking wet, on a patch of grass behind an office block. Unable to find a way off the industrial estate, that seemed to go on forever. Trying to find a shop to buy food. Trying to push through even when the wheels had come off.

I can remember eventually finding a hotel from a phonebook at a kiosk. Convincing the owner to accept English money. Soaking wet, starving, and deprived of sleep. Crashing out in that tiny, dim room, then waking up in a panic. Running out into the night.

From then on I struggle to piece it together. I ended up in Amsterdam and a British fan, on holiday with her boyfriend, recognised me. I must have been a state by then. From what was later said, that fan wanted to help me but the boyfriend had no interest in being a footnote in some minor rock biography. She set me up in a hostel for a few days where I did nothing but sleep. She got in touch with people back home. With Bonny, who called Frankie.

I can't remember the woman's name. Only her dark, moist curls hanging over her face, and her voice as she kept asking me to remember a phone number. Any phone number.

Fever set in, and I couldn't give her what she wanted.

8

It was two in the morning when Sam got back from the cocktail with Bonny. The complex seemed deserted, the young family that had moved in next door silent for the first time. Bonny had insisted on Bloody Mary after Bloody Mary, but they hadn't encouraged her to open up. The drunker she got the more obtuse and wilfully enigmatic she became. Her one useful contribution was the invite she handed him for her exhibition, as she said goodbye. It was described as 'a unique performance of The National Grid's music', and was to take place tomorrow. Her National Grid pictures featured heavily on the embossed piece of card, which didn't specify what form the performance would take. The wording suggested that the band members would be involved.

There was a pile of post for Sam, and with a sinking heart he saw that two of the letters were addressed to him.

Why had Elsa not opened her post when she got back from the exhibition, he wondered? Where was she? The pink suitcase she had kept in the hallway was gone, along with her long overcoat. A navy blue Karen Millen number he had felt unconvinced she could afford.

He tore open the small brown envelope, and pulled out a single white postcard.

If you encroach upon someone else's life, expect them to encroach upon yours. Starting from now.

Sam had a faint memory of seeing online postcards Robert had also sent his fans, not so long ago. Could Robert have sent this?

He wished Elsa was around.

It was a struggle to push himself up to the bedroom. Elsa had now emptied some of the boxes, and hung one or two pictures up. She couldn't be much longer, he thought, reaching for his laptop. He was sure he wouldn't sleep until she'd returned.

Sam was only able to find online one or two images of postcards Robert sent to his fans. One had been reasonably well photographed. It contained the words, 'Looking forward to seeing you all in Hamburg. Best, Robert.'

Sam pulled out the latest threatening postcard. The sloping handwriting was similar to that of the image on the internet. Maybe they were from Robert. But on the image Robert had looped the tail of the 'g' in an ornate way. On the word 'warning' from the new postcard the 'g' was not looped at all. But how did Sam know for sure that the postcards online were genuine? He wished he had remembered where he'd put the first letter. That, at least, would allow for a more reliable comparison.

He closed the screen and was about to pull the sheets around him when a great crashing sound filled his right ear.

Sam threw himself onto the floor. For a moment he lay hunched there, expecting a further onslaught of noise. But there was nothing.

Nothing but a powerful silence.

He felt as if his heart might tear free from his moorings.

Sam stayed hidden, trying not to make a sound or move until the heave in his chest began to subside. But every breath seemed deafening, every movement enormous and clumsy.

Tentatively, he approached the window.

It had been torn open by half a brick, now lying on the carpet. The jagged hole was lit for a moment by the headlights of a passing car. The two spotlights blinded him, sawed over the wall, and faded.

Sam approached the window gradually, searching for a retreating figure. But there was none. Only the blue leaves of the trees opposite the house.

He only realized he had fallen asleep when the phone by the bed blazed to life. The sheets next to him were untouched, and the early morning sun darted aggressively through the jagged gash in the window. He tore off the handset.

'Elsa?'

'It's Camille,' the voice said.

He breathed out. 'Camille? Oh. Right.' He consciously softened his voice. 'How are you?'

'It's a bit early for me to call, I know.'

Her accent sounded slightly exaggerated.

'It's okay. Just getting my head together.'

'Not a great night's sleep?'

'You could say that. Just moved into a new place.'

'How lovely.'

'Not really. We got the biggest mortgage it's possible to get. From a company who're yet to play their part in the intimate relationship they promised we'd have with them.'

'Oh right. So you're in debt to them?'

'Unless Comrade Brown offers me some free social housing.'

He picked up the invitation to Bonny's exhibition, and fingered it.

'Plus I've had some threatening letters, and last night a brick was thrown through my window.'

'Oh. Who would do this?'

'Fans, I think. Not of me, of the band.'

'Why?'

'Trying to persuade me to leave Robert alone.'

'Oh my. Well, it's not been great here either.'

'Why not?'

'Well... Martin is just the least supportive boss ever. He doesn't seem to understand what it's like to be new to England. It's not like in the movies at all.'

Sam laughed, wiping his eyes. 'Well, yeah. He should be sympathetic. Help you to settle in. I can't imagine what's it's like to start again in a new country. It's hard enough trying to start a career again.'

'Sure. When he employed me it was all about how he liked my love of music. But now he mocks that. You know, 'You thought you'd be having tea with Sting every Wednesday, didn't you, Camille?''

'The twat.'

'I know, I don't even like Sting.'

'Who does? I always preferred The Police.'

'Sam, he wants me to give you a push about finding Wardner. Mason House have had some hate mail off fans and he's worried that if they turn, the company will lose all its credibility. He takes that very seriously, you know.'

'What do you mean?'

'Well, he has no talent. This fictional idea of his street cred is very important to him. London's like Paris. You lose this quality and you're...'

'Toast?'

She laughed, as he sat up.

'He's ridiculous,' she said, dropping her voice. 'He shouted at a cleaner today for using bleach in the building, said it was terrible for our environment. But I see him driving through central London in a Land Rover all the time.'

'A Chelsea Tractor, we call it.'

'His wife's a counsellor. Her main ambition is to start a commune to 'protect us all from the psychological enslavement of living in a society', apparently.'

'You are joking.'

'No. Straight up. As Londoners say. So are you getting any closer to finding Wardner, then?'

'I got to interview Bonny yesterday and...'

'No way! I used to try and copy her fringe with blunt scissors.'

'Why didn't you use sharp ones?'

'I don't know.'

He crouched down on the floor. 'It was crazy.'

'I have to hear it. Say you taped it.'

'Of course. It was one of the strangest experiences of my life. She certainly knows more about Wardner than she's letting on.'

'God. I envy you, Sam, meeting people like that.'

'Have you heard about this exhibition of Bonny's paintings?'

'I read an article about it just now. Is her work any good?'

'Yes. I think she's actually very talented.' He sat up. 'But the pictures were strange. A lot of them depicted Robert, and seemed to have hidden messages in them.'

'That is so weird.'

'It looks like the event will double as a performance of some kind. We should go. I could ask Bonny if you can join me?'

'Go together?'

'Yes. Why not?'

'Okay. Only thing is, what if Wardner does show up? With his fans there, might they turn on you?'

Afterwards, Sam tore a panel from one of Elsa's cardboard boxes and taped it over the shattered panel. Standing by the window, he turned his phone on. Almost immediately a message from her flashed up:

Hey. Didn't want to get in the way of your fun night out. Malcolm asked me to meet some buyers who want to invest in the gallery. So staying at this exhibition in a hotel in Northumbria for a day or two. Got a rubbish signal. Will see you when I get back x

ROBERT WARDNER

The next memory is being back in England.

On a stiff bed, my body twisted into a weird position. A man in a woolly jumper asking me to sign a form.

I feel woozy and my bones ache. There's this pain in my stomach that could get overpowering any second. An Indian nurse with a harelip standing just behind the man, saying 'It doesn't matter, we'll have to do it without his consent.' Closing my eyes and trying to sleep.

They eventually leave.

I open my eyes and try to focus on my surroundings.

I'm in a small room with many pipes on the wall, painted this queasy shade of green. I stand up. Though I've got no idea where I am, the muggy warmth of the place seems familiar. Familiar in my gut and bones.

I go outside, into an empty hallway. It's like I'm sleepwalking. The hallway is lined with windows and I see that I'm one floor up. Outside, bare trees resist the hard London rain. I press myself up against the glass. Beyond that it's more streets, winding on and on. I'm trapped on the edge of one of them.

I struggle to follow a train of thought. When I snatch at a thought it's gone. People always seem to want something from me that's overdue, but when I work out how to give it to them, they're gone.

At first people don't disturb me much, except to occasionally make me eat chicken soup. It always comes with a soft white roll and a smudged portion of Flora. I tell them I'm a vegetarian. But when one night I'm brought steak and chips, I devour it.

Coronation Street *is playing on the TV in the dayroom and having eaten a square meal, the pictures on the screen make me feel alive again. I never thought that the sight of northern streets would make me feel invigorated, but it does. I suddenly miss the pub crowd at last orders, the shrill sound of the jukebox. The sense of claustrophobia that I finally kicked a hole in when I got a record deal.*

Every afternoon a young bloke with a clipboard comes and knocks on my door, even if it's open. He's always out of breath, and I always wonder what the rush is. He wears a tight camel-coloured shirt and shiny trousers and he stammers when he talks. Every day he asks me questions. How did I get here, where do I live? Although I can never be bothered, and I just guess most of the answers, he always seems to have been expecting whatever I say.

One day the Indian nurse calls him out of the room and he leaves his clipboard on the table next to me, half-filled out. At the top of it are the words 'Galveston Orientation and Amensia Test'.

Next to it I see someone has scribbled my name in thick pencil, and the words, 'nervous breakdown causing prolonged disorientation. Head injury?'

I'd almost got myself in a routine by the time Frankie came to visit me. Some nights, while the TV buzzed and the rain hummed outside, I'd try to piece it all together and I'd feel this massive hollowness inside. I'd try to focus on it, and it would always come with Frankie's face. I've got to call her, I'd think, but then I'd get too tired. I'd try to fight the tiredness, terrified that I might forget her.

I suspect that if Frankie had not visited me I would have eventually lost all sense of myself.

The African woman at reception had told me my wife was coming to see me tonight. She worked beneath a hoop of silver tinsel, reindeer antlers sat on top of hair. I wasn't sure if I'd dreamt her telling me that though, so was surprised that evening to see Frankie standing at the front desk, talking to her.

I recognised her poise way before I recognised her face.

'Jingle Bells' was playing quietly on the record player. Frankie's white skin shone against the shabby Christmas décor.

She was wearing a grey mackintosh and holding a small purse, shiny as a coin. I remembered that in times of stress she often held it close to her like a child's rag. Despite what I've put her through, she's blossomed, I thought.

The receptionist was looking for my file in the stack in front of her.

As I made my way closer to Frankie she turned. A lock of her long hair, darker than before, hid the bottom half of her face.

I heard her say to the receptionist 'Don't worry about it. He's here.' But she put her head down and squeezed the purse.

We stood opposite one another. She pulled the purse around and lifted her chin high, and it stopped me from speaking. She wasn't meeting my eye. I remembered how fine her features were.

'Where do we go then?' she asked, to no one in particular. The receptionist got to her feet.

'You'll have to use Mr Wardner's room if you want any privacy, darling,' she said.

'Sounds good,' I whispered.

I caught a glimpse of my robe, my slender legs, my pale white hands. Gripping the mike, they always looked more muscular.

As I looked for her approval I saw that her eyes had moistened. I grabbed her hand and to my surprise, after a moment of hesitating, she allowed it to fit gently inside mine. Small and quivering.

I led her to my room. The stooped, unshaven man and the refined, slender woman. He was no longer a pop star, in his pomp and glory, pulling her around backstage and she was no longer a nervous girl pretending to be worldly. She was everything I'd hoped she would become.

As soon as the door shut behind us she opened her mouth. But to my surprise no words came out. It was just this blank gasp. Her painted hand went to her forehead. 'Robert,' she said, firmly. Summoning up my courage I moved to take her in my arms. My trembling, dry hands trying to find the blend of softness and bone that secretly defined her to me.

Frankie allowed herself to be held, allowed herself to shimmer in my hands. But something was retained. She stayed stiff, distant. As I parted from her she kissed my cheek, and I felt a moist patch left there by her eyes. When I looked at her again, the air was sucked out of my lungs.

It's too late, I thought. This is just a sympathy call. Because she's a good person, who I once, almost, deserved. Until I abandoned her, because I couldn't handle my own failure. Going off to hide with weird Greek women who need something I can't give. Wandering round cities, sleeping rough while she was at home waiting for me. Just wanting everything to be alright again.

With tears smearing her mascara, she was more devastating than even I had remembered.

'This is my room then,' I said, with no idea of where to begin.

She looked around for a moment, and then up to the ceiling. 'You got back to England alright?'

'Yes.' I had committed to sitting in the chair while she stayed stood against the door. But it seemed a long way away, and it took me ages to settle into. I realized how daft that dynamic was, and leant forward towards her. Tried to compose myself, be manly. Yet whenever she looked at me she seemed overcome with emotion.

'How have you been?'

She laughed, and looked away. 'I've been...' she smiled, and very slowly made her way over to the chair at my side. 'I've been worried sick, Rob.'

She took my hand. I was relieved to see that it had almost completely stopped shaking. 'I'm so glad to see you're okay,' she urged, her voice faltering. 'But, Robert, I will never understand why you felt you had to run away from me like that.'

I looked down at the floor. Suddenly I was jolted from the fog that had clouded my brain for so long. I felt clear and composed. That single emotion she provoked was a powerful, guiding force.

It cut through everything.

'It was all I could do to try and stay sane. But you deserved much better. I wish I hadn't left.'

She offered a bruised smile.

'You were with another woman, weren't you?'

'Not like that. It was a friend.'

'That singer?'

'Yeah.'

She shook her head. With the pristine glow of her makeup she was too immaculate.

'So what's she got that I haven't?'

'Nothing. It was just, she's in the same game as me.'

'You're not in that game any more. So I guess you don't need her now?'

'It wasn't like that. After a bit, she didn't want me to go. I started to think she didn't want me going back to you, that she'd begun to want us to be more than friends. That was when she overstepped the mark.'

'What happened?'

'I had to get her out of my life. Fast. I knew I couldn't do anything that would end it with us.'

She looks up.

'I don't know what sort of logic that is, Robert.'

'I know.'

'Bonny really isn't happy about it. Says she put you two in touch. She feels a bit betrayed that the girl kept you hidden from her.'

'I just wanted to get my head right.'

She looked at me, but seemed to decide to leave it.

'I know you did,' she said, and she held my other hand.

'I'll get better,' I said. 'I'll be there for you again. I can do it. They can't keep me in here forever.'

Gradually, I felt her begin to tremble again.

9

As Sam ascended the escalators at Liverpool Street Station he couldn't find the hopeful, enthusiastic woman he'd met amongst the crowd before him. Until he realized that Camille was the woman in the black pleated leather dress. It clung to her taut torso, ending in a hard collar. With the glossy, shining material and her bright red lips she looked like the exotic hostess of a Berlin nightclub.

'Like the jacket, Mr Pop Star,' she said as he kissed her cheek. Her red nails flashed up to grasp his shoulder, her leather clinging momentarily to his. 'You look sharp.'

Sam felt embarrassed by his tattered leather jacket, bought years ago to mimic the one Wardner had once worn on *Top Of The Pops*. Not the night to wear it, he thought.

'There's quite a crowd gathering outside the venue. There's rumours that some of the band are going to play. Even that Wardner will sing for the first time since he vanished.'

The gallery was only a short walk through Spitalfield market, where stalls were now packing up for the day. Chic shop assistants, with Fred Perry shirts and neon hair, snapped chairs and tables shut around them. Sam felt in no mood to rush, walking beside this vision. 'You mean I'm about to be confronted with a legion of National Grid fans?' he asked.

She smiled, slowly. 'Well wouldn't you expect that? I suppose that the fans don't normally get the chance to meet up. Why so scared?'

'I'm not scared.'

'Come on,' she said.

Camille had been right. The gallery, on the side of the market facing the street, looked as if it had rarely contained more than a couple of fashionable passers-by. But tonight the whole lane was full of fans. An intense pantomime of fur-lined leather jackets.

They all had darkened eyes, eyes that seemed to have a hunger behind them. Borne out of the private convulsions only secret passions can provoke.

Many of them were teenagers, unborn when Wardner manhandled Julio Iglesias. Latex clung to young thighs, and hairspray wafted. Many were clad in box-fresh National Grid t-shirts. Sam had seen them sold at the station. They seemed a world away from that lone *Top Of The Pops* performance, with its ludicrous anger and odd foam pillars.

'You're a fan of the band too,' she said.

'I certainly was,' Sam answered. 'Hard to be as devoted when my home's getting gradually broken into, though.'

Camille took his hand. He held it gently, cherishing the contact. 'Have HMV just brought out a range of National Grid t-shirts?'

'It was Topshop,' Camille whispered, her red lips hidden behind her hand.

A couple of the more glamorous fans parted for Camille as they opened the glass door. Sam thought he saw a glimpse of Vicente, the producer, dressed in an all-white suit and brandishing a cane. Inside were the more seasoned gallery dwellers, in blazers and pashminas, surprised and frightened by this new influx. Behind the building crowd, on a small raised platform, was a makeshift stage. A keyboard, microphone stand and black guitar were visible.

Camille was taken aback by the artwork. 'My god, this is going to cause a sensation.'

'Exactly what their manager would want,' he replied.

True to form, Bonny, in a pinstriped navy suit, was surrounded by a swarm of journalists.

'So these pictures tell us how Wardner vanished, then?' one journalist asked, putting a microphone onto Bonny.

'Well, clearly, they are meant to capture my sympathy for his plight,' she said. 'Robert felt driven out of the world by commercial pressure. These pictures show his moment of liberation.'

'What do you say to the criticisms that you are using Robert's dark past to further your own career?' One journalist had clearly not done his homework on her.

Her eyes flashed. 'Tell me, darling, have you never heard of post-structuralism? Were you there at the moment that every news story you reported on broke? Are you trying to tell me you've never reproduced anything, just constantly created thrilling content? I've made a living nurturing talent, appreciating it. Not bitching at people who do something with it.'

A few fans cheered.

Another journalist piped up, an older man with a more languorous tone. 'Is it true this is just a part of Robert's publicity campaign for their next release?'

'Oh no,' Bonny said. 'This stage set just fell out of the sky and we thought we might as well use them for a knees up. Look, I am happy to answer sensible questions, but I won't be answering any on Robert's behalf. You will have to put them to him.'

'And will he be appearing tonight?'

At the moment this question was asked, Sam became conscious of fans in two black leather jackets craning in behind him. They creaked in anticipation.

'There will be a performance from members of The National Grid,' Bonny said. 'And the more astute amongst you will have noticed the stage behind me. And afterwards, Theo will be DJing.'

'Is it true that this is going to be the first set by The National Grid in twenty five years?' one asked.

'Wardner's coming tonight,' a voice behind Sam said. 'There's no way a microphone would be set up if he wasn't.'

'No, Robert Wardner will not be performing this evening,' Bonny announced.

'Is he scared he'll be arrested?' someone shouted.

Bonny ignored the question. 'However, other members of the original line-up will.'

'Does that having anything to do with this new book about Wardner, Miss Crawford?' the older journalist asked.

Bonny looked straight at Sam. 'Samuel's book about the band has my full endorsement,' she said.

'But not Robert's, evidently,' one fan hissed.

'Sam,' Bonny said, taking the crook of his arm. 'Stick around for the after party. I have something for you. Or perhaps I should I say, someone.'

Suddenly, tightly-packed elbows started to grow restless and someone screamed. 'It's Theo!'

'I see,' a tall fan with a quiff intoned. 'It's Theo and his band performing. Hardly a National Grid reunion.'

'Well, Wardner's too scared to come,' his partner said.

'I wonder who could possibly have scared him off?'

Sam tried to see through the bodies.

'You're the journalist who's been trying to track down Wardner, aren't you?' the man said. 'Behind that awful book?'

Sam looked urgently for the right person to address.

'No one's scaring anyone off,' Bonny said. 'Theo's going to be performing songs from the album.'

'No one's going to be singing Wardner's parts, are they?' the man asked.

'No,' Bonny said. 'Theo is going to be performing his parts, along with the original keyboardist. The rest, including Wardner's voice, will come from pre-recordings.'

'National Grid karaoke!' the female fan cried.

'This is a disgrace,' another wailed.

Consternation turned quickly to excitement as Sam recognised Theo's shark-like grin in the crowd. Fans cornered him from all sides, waving CD's and pens. 'You want me to sign your cleavage?' he said, to a fan. 'It was Camus paperbacks in my day.'

The slender creature of the night Sam remembered from their

glory days had morphed into a committed decadent. Theo was a skinny scarecrow made of shredded leather, crinkled eyeliner and chipped nail varnish. There was an element of Keith Richards about him. Fans pushed objects into his hands and grappled to ruffle his hair. 'Can you get Robert to perform again?' one asked.

'I can do very little, but music can do everything,' he answered. Bonny grasped his arm and pushed him to the stage.

'Who wants to hear some National Grid?' he boomed, into the mike.

A huge cheer filled the gallery. Bodies surged forward.

'Is he going to sing?' someone asked. 'God help us!'

Sam picked his way through the crowd, to Camille. 'I'm glad we didn't miss this,' she said.

'It's all a bit second-hand, don't you think?'

'Sure, but don't take it all so seriously!'

'If only Wardner would turn up.'

'Can you imagine if he did? He'd be crushed in seconds! Far better to stoke the excitement, for the big comeback.'

The screen above the stage flickered to life, a huge roar greeting the first sight of Wardner. Sam couldn't take his eyes off him, he seemed to move like an alien. It was as if he hadn't learn to walk, move, or express himself by watching others at all. Every movement was his own, incomparable. It was footage from a live performance of theirs from 1981, of 'World Of Neon'.

Sam and Camille pushed onto their tiptoes, unable to resist the excitement. Theo strapped on his bass, and motioned to a keyboardist. Soon the room filled with the sound of National Grid synths. 'He's off the tablets, then,' Camille said, watching him press the keys.

'Archive footage now filling the role of the absent,' a photographer said, trying to get a shot of the stage.

Wardner, his anger now dissolved in pixels, raged above their heads. Simon's jagged guitar lines were sorely missed, leaving an aching chasm in the arrangements.

Where is he, Sam wondered? Refusing this charade out of loyalty to Wardner?

Yet despite these absences, Sam felt his heart soar as Theo wheeled about the stage, his bass guitar scything invisible shapes in the air. They seemed to stay carved in it even when the song faded. The final notes were greeted with a slavish roar.

'No Wardner, then,' said a fan at his side, pouting through black lipstick.

She glared at Sam. 'Wonder whose fault that is?'

'Leave him alone,' a female voice replied.

Sam saw that just behind him was a woman with long dark hair and olive skin. Her flowing white dress a soft contrast against the leather terrain of the crowd.

'Wardner would be thrilled to hear he's worthy of a book,' she said, with a smile. She had a sophistication that Sam found soothing.

Sam smiled. 'It's kind of you to say that.'

'He has devoted fans,' she continued, in a calm, low voice. 'But they are like flies at a window. No more intelligent, either. Despite what they think.'

'Thank you, very much, er...'

'Nataly,' she said.

ROBERT WARDNER

I'm in Manchester, waiting for Simon. Looking down The Northern Quarter.

It's all murals and fake bistros in 2007. Like you can have an authentic Italian experience sat next to the latest building site. We've raised a generation of professional liars.

February 1971 did it. Built a new layer that some knob heads fell for.

There's a real Manchester under all this, bulging to get out. The Manchester that I know, waiting for buses, once they call time at the Night And Day. A hard rain's going to fall, and then we'll find out what it's made of.

When I squint upwards, I see Simon coming from the London Road. Wait for him to come to me.

'You alright, kid?'

'I'm about to get drenched. I don't want to hang about here all day.'

'Jesus, Rob, you look like you've been to hell.'

'Worse. London.'

'Good to see you, fella. Brian said he was going to wait out here at eleven sharp. But as usual, the wanker's late.'

I kick at the floor.

'Here he is.'

Simon takes me to the glass door of the studio. It could be a wine bar for all I know. One big espresso machine, built into the wall.

We walk into this Perspex reception area. With what looks like a rabbit warren coming off it. Manchester's ripped sky in the dirty windows. 'So glad you've chosen our studio to kick things off again, Mr Wardner,' Brian says.

I need a smoke before anything's going to get done.

A kid with a Mohawk grabs my elbow. 'It's Robert Wardner!' he says. Grabs his brother, some milk sop in a cagoule. 'Ere, come and look at this. Him from The National Grid. It is you, isn't it?'

Simon comes between. 'Come on, not now. He's only just got inside.'

This Brian makes his presence known. He's a modern entrepreneur, you know.

'Here,' he begins, getting the kid's ear. 'This studio is a sanctuary. You respect this man's privacy, understand? You tell any of your daft mates he's about and you're barred from recording here an' all. That goes for all of you.'

'He gets it,' the milk sop says. I saw him play keyboards once, he was like Mozart. Probably had private lessons from the age of two.

'We heard you were recording here, Mr Wardner, but we didn't quite believe it. Did we? That's a tenner you owe me, Stew,' he says, turning to his side.

'Come on,' Simon says.

'You his guitarist? We been trying to rip off that sound you had, on 'State Of Exile'. How did you do it?'

'You think I'll give that away for free, son?'

'Come on, tell us. You could produce our record.'

'You hear that Simon?' I say. 'You're the next George Martin.'

'Robert, will you sign something for me? My drum sticks? Anything? It's Robert Wardner!'

'Yeah, not John Lennon.'

'It's okay, Si. Yeah, alright kid,' I say.

They always want more, normally. But these kids seem alright. Probably more discarded Joy Division basslines under some rent-a-gob frontman.

'He doesn't want to hang around here forever,' Brian said.

'He doesn't want his collar felt,' some kid joked. Simon pretended not to hear it.

It was good to get in the studio. Locked away. Nothing had changed. Just the words on the kit. It's still attention seekers, surrounded by expensive toys.

I get a flashback of sitting at a piano. Simon takes the master recordings out of his bag. 'Bonny dropped these off to me this morning.'

'How is she?'

'She's an artist now.'

'Course she is.'

I sit myself at the Korg behind the mixing desk. Simon hasn't filled the space on the other side of the screen with musos this time. Easing me in, I reckon.

I fire it up.

My fingers crackle. Find my way into this line of notes I was playing last time. Soon, it flows.

'Jesus. You got a name for that?'

I turn up the reverb a bit. 'You remember that time we saw the Arndale Centre getting replaced? You remember how the sound was inside there?'

'Yeah. So?'

'There was this kid's arcade ride they put outside the Woolworths. When you walked past the centre, you could hear it in the distance. Still can't forget it.'

'Hang on. I'll get my guitar.'

He runs to his case in the corner.

We play.

He always looks like he was born cradling a guitar. I think about being onstage in Hamburg, flat on my back, when my voice gave out. Him doing this solo that tore the sky open. Thinking, when did he learn that?

He finds me. Whatever quirks I take him on, he accommodates. E minor, F# minor, G# minor, A minor, B. He makes this musical shudder round it. Soon, a melody begins to crackle through me. Something awakens in me.

Simon turns around, smiling. 'Could be something,' he says.

Through the shaded glass panel on the door I can see youths, steaming it up. Clamouring.

'Ignore them.'

'How do they know I'm here?'

'I haven't told anyone.'

'Really?'

'Course not. We don't want the wrong people sniffing about.'

Simon kneels over the control panel, flicks some switches. After a pause he says, 'I told Theo. Let's start with 'World Of Neon'. It's a decent way in.'

I move over to inspect the speakers.

'You told Theo? Why didn't you just call Manchester Evening News?'

'I thought he'd keep it to himself.'

'And the rest.'

The speakers are thick with dust. I run a finger along them.

'What is it, Rob?'

'These speakers. They've had it.'

'They'll do the trick.'

'The album's too big. We can't finish it now.'

'They're fine. Don't start. 'Ere, Rob. 'World Of Neon'. Let's familiarize ourselves, eh?'

I flick a switch on one of the smaller synths.

It isn't plugged in.

'We don't have to re-record it,' he says. 'Just treat it.'

'What?' I shake my head. 'I'm not trying to get on Pop Idol. I've not got the teeth.'

'Or we could start with the drums?'

Over the PA a kick-drum batters my ears. Soon the walls are shaking with the nagging, crushingly familiar drum sound.

Still sounds like the future.

'Just bringing the rest up,' he says.

This is like that bloody exposure therapy.

'Where are you going?' he asks.

'To meet my fanbase, where do you think?'

'Seriously Rob, what's up?'

'You think I can work with a fuckin' scout troupe trying to get in the door?'

'I'll have a word with Theo. He just got over-excited, told a few journalists. You saying you didn't tell anyone you were going to work with us again?'

'Wanted to keep a low profile.'

'Well who else knows you're around? Frankie?'

'Course not.'

'Nataly?'

There's a twitch on the back of my neck.

'Don't ever talk about Nataly.'

He raises his chin. Views me from the corner of his eyes.

'She is still around then?'

'Why?'

'No. It's just. I hear some of the fans online pretend to be her. Why were you so angry with her?'

'I wasn't. Anyway, out of anyone, who are you to question me? You're the one who told Theo I was back. That's why we're going to get hounded. Can't believe you couldn't keep it to yourself.'

'Rob, come on.'

'Nah, you do what you've got to do. But this is all too soon for me. I need to get out of the city.'

'You're not leaving.'

'It's too far gone, Simon.'

I put my hand on the door knob.

'It's not. What about the label? It's just a bunch of young lads. A cooperative. You're not going to blow it for them are you?'

'Yeah, I'm going to hang about for a record label, with all they've done for me. With any luck we can conduct a séance and resurrect Cunningham. Get him involved. It's not worth putting our hands in now.'

He reaches for the doorknob. With this force that surprises me he screws my hand off it.

'Stay, Rob.'

He holds my gaze.

'Why?'

'I can't do it on my own.'

'I'm sorry, mate. But all this is behind me now. Besides, you heard that kid outside. It's you who made that sound, not me. You could teach *a whole new generation. But I'm getting out. Right out of all this.'*

'You think I'm following you back up the river, Kurtz? You got another thing coming.'

I open the door.

'See you.'

10

The set was short, a few album tracks but no big hits. Theo was slow to leave the stage, but Bonny motioned to a technician, who cut the sound. She took the mike, as Theo reluctantly removed his bass.

'We are delighted that so many of you still care about The National Grid,' she said, feedback hissing from the monitor.

'I'm not sure I do,' a journalist said to an accomplice, by Sam's shoulder. He was twirling his grey goatee. 'I'm just curious about whether we've just been forced to watch a song performed by a murderer, or not.'

'We love you, Bonny!' came a shout.

Bonny blushed, rather professionally, Sam thought. 'We love you too,' she said. 'And of course, this is just a taster of what is to come. Over the next few months the band are finally finishing off the album that we all hold so dear to our hearts. Mr Robert Wardner will be involved, and I envisage that you will soon be hearing these songs performed by all of the members.'

Sam noticed Theo laughing.

'Bonny,' a journalist shouted. 'Can you say for certain that Wardner will be performing again, given these rumours of an impending arrest?'

'What I can say for certain is that this is a performance and an art exhibition, not a press conference. But watch this space,' she said, waving her glass before moving to depart the stage. She snapped back the microphone once more. 'And buy my paintings!' she shouted, to a slightly bloodless cheer.

Sam noticed her expression instantly harden, as she motioned with a finger across her throat to the sound technician. Stagehands started to remove the equipment.

In lieu of Wardner, the crowd expressed their excess excitement on the paintings. With mischievous eyes, Sam and

Camille assumed a position against the end of the wall on which pictures were mounted.

A black-lipsticked woman and her partner jostled for a view of them.

'Everyone knows Wardner didn't escape to Europe. That was the whole reason he left a copy of *Passage To India* on his bed,' the man announced.

'It wasn't *Passage to India*, came the riposte. 'It was Jean Genet's *Our Lady Of The Flowers*. I think it was his way of telling us he was going to hide in Paris.'

'He'd have been recognised in Paris, don't you think? The LP went gold over there.'

A woman with purple hair had been biding her time to speak. 'Not if a suicide attempt had damaged his face.'

Camille rolled her eyes.

Sam was relieved to see he wasn't alone in taking the band too seriously.

'One thing's for sure,' the man said, craning in. 'Bonny has a new future.'

'Well if so, why are the band even involved?' came a reply.

They stood for a moment, facing the pictures in a reverent semi-circle. Sam considered the picture, the slight ache of the sombre colours, the way that the etched words blended into one another. A flowing sea of messages.

'Theo might know where he is.' Camille said.

The bassist had now undone his jacket, a thin sheen of sweat visible on his brow. He clasped a glass of champagne tight in his fist. 'But my dear, champagne is the true drink of the socialist,' he was saying, to a young journalist. 'Ask any of the New Labour cabinet, even now Blair's abandoned ship.'

The fans hadn't dispersed: merely coagulated around the entrance. Waiting for something to happen. Bonny had clearly trained the staff to push them towards her paintings, as the usual crowd seemed reticent. The fans are waiting for me to leave so they can get me, Sam thought. Camille's arm brushed his and he wondered if it was a sympathetic reflex, or something more.

The crowd gathered round Theo, and Sam noticed a change in his manner. He could see the louche socialite he remembered gradually emerge from the past. Theo caught his eye.

'Is there any chance you could sign this?' a fan asked. 'Could you put something wise on it?'

Theo scribbled.

'Autographs are pointless,' the fan said, reading it out. 'Brilliant.'

'You were amazing,' another fan fawned. 'Are you touring any time soon?'

'No. I have this dream of playing a gig at which there is no music, no audience, and no performance. If we can ensure we're dead as well we'll be as famous as God.'

'Is it strange performing in front of a video of Robert?' Camille asked him. Theo passed back a pen and considered her slowly.

'Nothing is strange these days, darling. Everything is permitted. Now. What a gorgeous dress you are wearing.'

Camille raised her hand to the leather above her cleavage. The dress shimmered, one long illumination that shook up a pleat in her skirt and dispersed around the fabric at her neck. 'Thank you,' she said.

'A friend of yours?' Bonny asked, looming over to Theo.

'Bonny, this is Camille, who also works for my publisher,' Sam said.

'Ah, Mason House. You're the guy who's writing the book on us, aren't you?' Theo asked.

Sam felt several sets of eyes shift onto him.

'That's right,' he said. 'I was hoping Wardner would be here, to give us his side of the story.'

'You've scared him off,' a voice behind them said.

Theo's eyes moved from Camille and bobbed onto Sam's face

for a moment. He leant in. He smelt of expensive aftershave and cheap chemicals, but Sam could still see him seducing a young fan. 'We should have a drink, after my set,' Theo said. 'You can tell me how close you are to finding him.'

'I was hoping you could tell me that. I have no idea.'

'Sign our bodies first, Theo!' shouted a girl wearing a miniature top hat.

In the nightclub Sam could see a slender woman, in black tights and a corset, climbing a ribbon towards the ceiling. As he ascended the stairs and walked in, a blast of sound hit his ears. Camille followed behind him, the second meaning of her black leather unleashed by synthetic beats and close dancing. Sam marvelled at how easily people walked off the street and into these decadent dioramas. It was spooky how easily people's inner landscapes were expressed in enclosed booths and glittering bars. Their private nightmares slid into the moulded furniture as if it had been designed for them. People discovered a new sense of stasis in these places, Sam thought. A moral as well as social stasis. He thought it fitting that the music was bloodless electro, as affectless as the cities in which it was created. Sam felt for the phone in his pocket, and set it to vibrate. Would he feel it if Elsa replied, he wondered? He was dreading the caustic reply he'd get when she read that he'd gone to London.

Bodies half-turned towards him, sleeked in sweat. Camille's hand snaked around his arm. Her leather stuck to his and all the activity around them seemed unable to separate it. As he turned to her she pointed up the stairs. 'Bonny said he'd be up there,' she said. 'Recovering from the strain of having spun records for twenty minutes.'

Sam pushed through the dance floor to the elevated seating. The proximity of Camille's leather-clad body made him feel debauched. All around limbs parted, their mechanical movements embodied by something he couldn't see. The white strobe shivered over each frame. Everyone's flesh shone, the crowd one oscillating body that moved like a shoal of fish. On the crest of each wave the sparkle of jewellery, the shimmer of latex, the lustre of sprayed hair. Private agonies finding their only outlet through intense, idiosyncratic dancing.

As he pushed through Sam noticed fingers poking into bags of white powder. Latex tights, the arch of their gloss rising in silver arcs as women danced. Sam stooped over, clutching his jacket around him. Marilyn Manson's 'Great Big White World' chattered into its chorus, the thick, treated noise sweeping him along. Sam looked up. His eyes were met by a profile he recognised, veiled in red light.

Wordlessly, Theo motioned them up to his table. They pushed past the coupling bodies towards it. There, Theo was sat on a couch, holding court. 'You two,' he said, waving them over with a fey hand.

From the ceiling the woman spun down the thick ribbon, her slim body uncoiling it. Below her, the crowd gasped its appreciation. Her legs sawed at the lowest point as she gathered the ribbon around her torso again, like a spinning top. Strobes flickered over her clenched thigh muscles, her burning eyes, her glittering hair. Her carefully honed talent a cheap buffet people gorged on at will.

As Sam looked for a place to sit he noticed something about the people around Theo. They each had over-earnest expression, and occasionally they looked down guiltily. There was a chemical pinch to the air, a sense of conspiracy. At the centre of it was Theo's fixed smile, scanning over it all. The two of them sat down opposite him. 'So,' he said, leaning forward. 'What did you think of my set?'

'I never thought I'd hear Throbbing Gristle played in a club.'

'I'm embracing my new image. I'm going to be the next John Peel, but with better hair. Wasn't his hairdo rubbish? No wonder he was on radio. Don't you find it strange? You can make a whole new career, based on a few quips you once made on national television.'

'Lives turn on such moments,' Sam said.

'Indeed. So, Bonny tells me that you're desperate to find Robert?'

Sam looked at Camille. 'Yes, I suppose that's true.'

His eyes skittered over Sam, black eyeliner crumbling in the corners.

'So do you think you'll succeed?'

'With the help of people like you, maybe.'

He held Sam's gaze for a second too long.

'I see,' he said. 'But first thing's first.'

At his side, a man pulled out a small bag of white pills and dipped his hand into it. Palmed the contents onto Theo. Theo looked around him, and then spread out his fingers. He held two white tablets, with the imprint of a dove upon them. 'So we're going on a journey together. Aren't we, Sam?'

A waitress in a baby-doll dress passed, placing bright cocktails in front of them. They teemed with mint leaves and crushed ice. 'Bottoms up?' Theo asked.

Camille looked carefully over at Sam.

'Want to take the trip or not, Sam?'

'I don't know.'

'You know where the door is, Sam,' Theo said.

He thought of the shards of glass on the carpet, as the car passed outside in the night. 'Let's do it,' he said, looking at Camille.

'Let's,' Camille echoed.

11

'Don't let him get in your head. He wasn't trying to mess with you. He was probably just having some fun,' Camille called. In that outfit, her dynamism made Sam mentally pair her with the lights. Dazzle and danger whirled around him, with all the worry of recent days now accelerated, expressed in a carnival of overwhelming stimuli.

'You're right,' Sam shouted, over sirens and keyboards. They dipped like rollercoasters, swerved into his senses like sharp corners on the track.

Everyone else was laughing as he watched Camille dance.

Theo stayed on the balcony, watching over proceedings. People bit their bottom lips and stamped to the industrial grind of the song. Has it kicked in yet, Sam wondered?

'Once we've partied for a bit he'll open up,' Camille shouted, sipping her cocktail. 'Let's have a good time.' She looked exhilarated, sensual.

Sam saw that the other people who'd also taken pills were now surrounding him. One by one, they were rolling up the bottom of their jeans to expose their calves.

They're out to get me, Sam thought. They're all in on it, and they know that the one person who doesn't roll up their trouser legs isn't one of them.

Camille was smiling, lolling her head back. He resented how easily she fell into a beautiful motion, while, like most men, he languished on a high bank of irony and fear.

She leant into him, her skin sleek. Cupped her hand over his ear. As she talked Sam imagined her lips moving, thick and moist. 'I think it's hitting me now,' she said, enjoying every consonant. He felt her thighs press against his, the fabric of her dress stretched as one long leg moved between his. Her arm curled behind his back, pulling her into him. It would be so easy,

Sam thought, for us to dance into a corner. For me to unbuckle the zip at her collar, and watch the tight leather peel from her hot flesh.

The chorus of the song swooped in, the digital crash of sound sweeping him along. Everyone continued their enclosed, suspicious dance. Sam felt a hissing in his blood, had the sense of something crumbling inside him and reaching up, with clammy, chemical fingers, to quiver in his veins. It shimmered around his hands and wrists, and danced through his fingertips.

'It's hitting me too,' he said.

Sam looked up to the balcony. It was empty.

Camille pulled him into her, the dance floor flooding as the music grew louder. For a moment Sam imagined her as the queen of a tribe, the raw appeal of her body drawing a rabid semi-circle of men to worship her. With the right soundtrack, he thought, they would all kneel down and kiss her heels.

Moments later she caught his eye, as if to say it was hitting her again. 'I'm going to enjoy this,' Sam thought. 'For a few moments of my life I don't have to worry. When this hits me, I can finally break free of it all.'

It was at that moment that the song peaked. Sam felt a pulsation at the back of his neck that pushed him into a cloud of pleasure, made him giddy with each throb. Each wave had an after-effect that attached to the first, until there was this joyous, bouncing Möbius Strip of sensation that charged him to lift his chest, raise his voice, celebrate. Men from the balcony put their arms round him and he looked at their laughing, grimacing faces and felt a kinship. A synthetic sense of safety. Camille joined hands with them too. He felt ecstatic. 'I'll tell her everything,' he thought. The drugs bubbled and fizzed in his body, making him pop out his legs, jaggedly splay his arms, whoop for pleasure whenever another chorus hit.

A woman grabbed him by the elbow. 'Got any MD?' she said. He shook his head. 'I want some MD,' she pleaded, pulling at his shirt.

Camille suddenly looked serious, and asked a man something. He nodded, pointed to the stairs. She motioned to Sam that she was going to have a cigarette. Did he want one?

The veranda was deserted, except for a hunched man, bizarrely absorbed by his calculator watch. 'I think I need some water,' Camille said. 'Is it just me, or do you want some water?'

'I want some clean air,' Sam said.

They sat down on the grated metal, looking up at the sky. Coldness pinched around them, a coldness serrated by the dispersion of the pill in his blood. Camille sparked up a cigarette and inhaled. 'Don't worry if you don't get to talk to Theo,' she said. She looked down, knocking the cigarette with a painted finger. 'You do know I think you're doing a great job?'

He looked up, and at that moment a plasticky joy hit his jaw. He felt as if his head was bobbing as another bustling wave cascaded through him. He heard his words come out, cool and deliberate. 'I am glad that you're around to help out with this. You know?'

She smiled, and looked down at the metal. 'I think you're going to make something really special.'

'You're helping me,' he said, charged by the way she smiled as he leant closer. 'You're encouraging me.'

She inhaled, and blew a plume of smoke upwards. 'No. You've encouraged me. Everyone else says I was stupid. Moving from my home to England for a load of bands that no longer exist.'

He could picture her clearly. Lost in a distant town. Trapped inside the porous boundaries of a book or record.

'Did you like Paris?'

She looked down at the floor. He wondered what mental riffs made her reflective expression so natural. He could imagine her as a teenager, spending whole summers inside the sleek interiors of Savage Garden albums. Wishing her life was more like that.

'Not towards the end,' she said. 'I'm still waiting for the London I'd heard about.'

'That doesn't matter. You can still find traces of it.'

She smiled. 'You know, that is true.'

'Course. It's impossible to prove how shaped we are by art we love. You have to live off the traces.' There was a knot in his stomach, born of a need to lift her mood.

She laughed. 'They are there, aren't they?' she said.

'I could take you to clubs in Manchester. Although most of them have been bulldozed over to make branches of Wetherspoons. But in some of them, just in certain corners, you can sense the musicians who danced there in their early days. It sounds mad, but sometimes I think I can almost experience the thoughts behind the songs I love.'

'I'd love to experience that. The teenage part of me is still looking for those things.'

'Then we will,' he said, putting his hand on the compressed leather of her arm. She didn't move it, and she smiled again. Slowly this time. He wanted to move his hands through the precise abandon of her hair. He thought of Elsa, and stopped himself. He felt painfully alone, but knew it would be extinguished with a kiss. Don't, he thought. Be genuine to Elsa. Without that clarity, nothing makes sense.

'I hope I'm still around when you finish this book,' she said.

She seemed to be considering whether to place her head on his shoulder, or snake her hand through his hair and kiss him. At that sensual moment any delicate trap felt courageous and right. Her perfume clouded round him, a seductive haze in which Sam felt anything could happen.

As she leant forward the harsh light of the balcony lit her hair. He felt her proximity, the fragile nourishment he knew he could glean from a kiss. Holding back felt cowardly, despite the memory of Elsa. But he reminded himself that he was not a character in a book, who would indulge for the whims of a reader.

She looked slowly away, as if amused at her predicament. 'That might be the last of it,' she said.

'Are you going to offer me some of that cigarette or what?'

She nodded. The plastic sensation was returning. He wanted to express something to her so directly that it would cut through all the confusion around them.

She coughed. The music inside grew louder. She licked her lips slowly.

'We should go back in,' he said.

It was almost four a.m. when the two of them found a seat in the McDonalds. Theo had proven elusive, escaping with two burlesque dancers in black corsets at three a.m.. They recognised the person who offered Camille a lift home from the balcony. One of the few fans who'd made it to the after-party. While the tendrils of the pill still soothed them it felt natural for Sam to join Camille for the ride. But the lift only took them as far as the outskirts of the city, leaving them at an all-night McDonalds near the motorway. As the euphoria of the night faded the two of them realized they would have to wait until the six a.m. bus to get to Camille's. Even as the buzz had retreated, it had left behind a fragile shell that they'd lingered in together. As the new morning had pressed through the lights from the car park, Sam realized how exposed his comedown would be. Soon the adrenalin would go, and the payback would begin.

He dreaded the moment this would occur, on a strange pop-up site spinning off the M25. Yet given his company something told him it would be painfully, synthetically beautiful.

He looked at the margin of their reflection in the window, and for a moment wondered if he could slip inside that silvery realm, be irretrievable. Permanently wrapped in the unique Lucite of the morning.

There were only a few people in the McDonalds. Half an hour ago a stag do had pounded on the Drive-Thru window, finding it closed before carving inside the restaurant. Their muscular bodies teemed with togas and testosterone. They had gathered on the table behind Sam as they sat down. Sam had tried to catch the sharp motifs of their in-jokes, punch lines spinning aimlessly as the discarded burger wrappers in the car park. Now they were gone they had permitted a cherished silence. With her hair ruffled, and lipstick dried to a narrow shade of decadence, Camille had gone into another realm. She looked as if she not only had all the answers, but as if she was tired of their aggregate weight.

Camille looked out at the strip-lit car park, the vehicles now like mini spaceships. She smiled. The smile seemed to acknowledge how painful the morning light would be. As he sucked at his Pepsi, Sam wondered if the wind had shifted outside. He felt as if his soul had been shrink-wrapped, prevented from familiar lunges of emotion, instead left to cower and wait. He succumbed to the hard edge of chemical coldness that sat inside him. Camille met his eyes and shivered.

When their meals came they could only poke at them.

The rush of the evening had awoken a sense of entitlement that felt so modern it was almost satisfying. At the counter they had both ordered swathes of cheeseburgers and fries but now they sat on the table, as if behind a plastic screen. The pill had, at one point, rendered everything delicious. But it had only taken a slight shift to show what a confidence trick that all was.

'I've never felt this cold before,' Camille said. 'I feel as if I've shrunk inside.'

'I know,' Sam replied. They looked out at the car park, beyond it the temporary lights of the city.

'Are you sad you didn't get to talk to Theo?' she asked, taking a sip with her bloodless lips.

Sam felt an urge to trace the side of her face with one finger, place a stray black lock into the rest of her hair. She recognised the impulse, indulging Sam with her eyes.

'I'm realizing that it doesn't ever seem to work like that. Perhaps I can't expect people to be so attainable.'

'I don't know,' she said, shaking the Pepsi. 'Perhaps we need more enigmatic figures. People who give us the room to work ourselves out while we go after them.'

'So in that case, finding Wardner would have a cost?'

She looked out of the window. 'I don't know. Are you not going to touch your food?'

'Not just now.'

'Don't blame you. This place isn't going to win any Michelin stars. I can't see Martin taking his wife here for an aperitif any time soon.'

As she looked out of the window Camille seemed to be looking through the car park, through the lights. Behind them. 'You alright?' he asked.

'I don't know.'

She inhaled, and held the breath. 'You see those dots on the horizon, Sam? I think all of them are like little universes, aren't they? Homes, cafes, nightclubs, cars. They move and switch on and off. From here they seem insignificant, temporary. It is barely worth following them because soon they will pop, pssh, and be gone.'

'So what if that's true?'

'Well, perhaps we are just like them?'

'Barely worth following?'

'Exactly. All this, the book. Trying to make sense of people's histories, what it all means. Everyone is looking to the past for answers, as if the blueprint was left there. But it's all just distant dots. Soon they will wink off too.'

Sam put down the Pepsi. 'I sometimes think about how we're all looking back. We should be trying to change the present, but people have become so reductive. Nowadays they seem only interested in money, sex and attention. In getting cheap laughs. When I was younger, I genuinely believed the future would be made in the margins.'

'The margins? The fringes of society?'

'The people who still believe in music.' He leant forward. 'I mean the margins where it's uncertain. That bit of room we have, where we decide how to behave. Those margins where interpretation and sensuality are. I used to believe we could use them to invent new lifestyles.'

'But how could we make that happen?' Her eyes narrowed, the long lashes trembling.

'By changing the script. By not acting as we're expected. At gigs, at parties, places like that. When I was young I thought people went with an open mind. I thought if one person there suggested using the furniture for a strange act of make-believe then everyone just joined in. I watched David Bowie on *Top Of The Pops* and thought, 'That is the spark.' I thought, 'From now on, people will relate to one another through personas. There'll be a sexual revolution.' But everyone just looks for the normal way to behave. Tries to find the agreed script, even if it doesn't really exist.'

'Not online though.'

'Online isn't real life. Not yet.'

'You're right. Wouldn't it be fun to stay in a hotel and just try out a new identity? See whether you prefer that one instead?'

'Exactly. Perhaps we should do that.'

She nodded, and looked out at those lights.

12

Elsa knew Malcolm was the sort of man who took pride in never appearing ruffled. But as he hurriedly threw shirts into a leather suitcase, a blaze of frustration flushed onto his face.

'You don't need to leave,' Elsa said.

He looked up, and she noticed he was panting a little. 'I set this up carefully,' he said. 'Some of the richest and most discerning art buyers in the world are, as we speak, milling around in the downstairs lobby. I wanted to introduce them to you this weekend. Yet for some bizarre reason you insist upon throwing all that back in my face.'

'Malcolm,' she said, 'I'm not saying I don't want that. It is wonderful, what you've set up here. Come on, look at how wonderful this setting is.'

He cast his eye, moodily, around the expansive hotel room. The suite large enough to have its own self-enclosed living room, complete with chandelier, glass tables and silk curtains. A fountain, that bubbled languorously though the bay windows. The child in him, she could see, was reluctant to leave. When had Sam ever offered this, she thought? This is a new world for me. She stepped closer to him.

'All I'm saying is that it's too soon for us to share a room together, as a couple. I've only just bought a house with Sam, and I can't blow all that away overnight. You have to give me time!'

'Right,' he said, smoothing his hair distractedly. 'So you're okay with the amenities, but don't want me to go near you while you enjoy them?'

'It's not that.'

He clenched his hands. 'When are you going to see, Elsa? Sam is an utterly pathetic loser.' He threw down the lid of the suitcase. 'Just take one look at him. He's never succeeded at anything in his life yet you've already wasted your best years on him. And yet still you spurn all this!'

'My best years? Malcolm, please.'

'No,' he said, seizing the case as sleeves flapped around the edges. 'You know, I intended for us to become business partners someday, Elsa. But you instead want to loaf around with that retarded adolescent.'

'Malcolm, stop it now.'

'I will see you at work on Monday morning.' He grasped the suitcase against him, and then turned and slammed the door.

She went to the lobby. Elsa saw through the window that Malcolm had left, the space where his BMW had sat now replaced by a silver Jaguar. At the reception, a sheikh received instructions from a concierge, who steered him into The Maple Suite. If Malcolm had stayed, Elsa thought, tonight I would have been in there too. Mingling with rich and influential buyers, and becoming a part of something enterprising.

I should not have come here in the first place, she decided. Last night was a mistake. Now I'm stuck in a hotel that only the spoilt can understand, with no way of getting home, and a phone with only a fleeting signal.

She stayed in the lobby, resending a carefully worded text to Sam until satisfied it would have reached him.

The concierge craned over her, and asked if he could help. As Elsa looked past him she recognised one or two faces from the Gavin Holding launch around her. They nodded in her direction, and Elsa wondered what they would make of her presence here. How do they remember me, she thought? For a moment she wondered if Bonny would soon appear amongst them.

'The pool is now open again madam, if you're interested?'

It was almost midnight by the time Elsa made her way down to the pool. The darkened room was empty, the low lights on the walls somehow disconsolate. She felt dirty, lost and desperate. I'll stay in here, she thought, until the water has cleansed every inch of Malcolm from me.

At the edge of the pool, Elsa dropped her gown. She caught a glimpse of her long, taut frame, clad only a bikini, in the sauna window opposite. Just before it was obscured by steam. But as she kept looking at her reflection she could not make out any of her features. The heat removed the image from that distant screen. It was as if Elsa had just vanished.

The water passed sleekly around her body and after a few long strokes she lay there, just under the surface of the water, her hair splayed in a white, ghostly swirl. She hung for as long as she could hold her breath. As she bobbed she felt glad to have shed her own movements, her own mannerisms, for a few moments. Breaking to the surface Elsa exhaled, placing her hands gently behind her head as she closed her eyes. She imagined the heat opening her pores. Cleansing her of her guilt.

The National Grid, Hulme Warehouse
14th September 1981

'Everything is falling apart,' Robert Wardner intones. A cymbal is dashed to the floor. Nerves are shredding. The band are throwing looks as sharp as cut glass at one another. The audience is willing the band through every moment. Lady Luck, it appears, is not.

The National Grid's final show of this tour is not at the Alexandra Palace. Or even at London Astoria. It is at Manchester's Hulme Warehouse. Despite the band's tattered emblem hanging defiantly behind them throughout, this is not the triumphant homecoming finale we all dreamed of.

It's something darker.

Greeted with devoted cheers, frontman Robert Wardner skulks around the drum kit, refusing to move to the front of the stage, or even look at the audience. When he does come forward hands reach out to touch him, but he looks at them as if they are images on a screen. On record he sings to us from another world, imparting concerns about hooded figures and bizarre rituals that we can barely comprehend. He is a man whose eyes have witnessed a thousand car crashes, but who remains too fragile to stand in front of traffic and demand it all stop. When he begins to sing into the microphone it is as if he is finally cracking under the burden of these songs. Each one requires nothing less than a total immersion of the self. But tonight the gods are raining down their bitterness upon him, denying him the opportunity.

During the opening number the drums never find their stride. Sticks slice at thin air as the bass drum goes awry. Cymbals seem out of reach, and are left static. Vital propulsive moments in 'We, The Workforce' are missed, and the keyboards, normally such a thick layer of sound, are left reedy by an amp that blows, with a heartrending 'phut', during the first verse.

Only a genius can force the audience to play a role in their performance. Rock music is most thrilling when we, the crowd, urge the musician to express what we cannot.

So it is tonight. Wardner has a light grip of his talent at the best of times, cowed by a responsibility to convey the otherworldly. Tonight we tear our throats raw with encouragement.

But Wardner is a doomed man. For him the moment has passed, and the stakes are too high. Only he can see the whole bargain, and he cannot convey the details to us, mere blips on his monitor.

'We've only got one working amp left,' guitarist Simon hisses into his mike. Theo's bass is slung too low for him, and our minds use that as justification for his muted notes. In 'Teleport', Simon slashes with such ferocity that he breaks two strings, tearing open the skin on his arms with the flailing wires. There are no guitars left intact from the tour and he kicks at Theo's amp in disgust. For a moment, all sound dies.

Wardner grasps the microphone, a pilot making one last announcement to the passengers before the plane plummets. 'Everything is falling apart,' he says, the reverb on his voice making this an infinite statement.

The bass amp makes a constant sawing plea from then on, panning from speaker to speaker, but there is life in it yet. It's the last Spitfire in the hangar. The gods of misfortune and hellfire have entered this desolate factory space in Greater Manchester, and we all swear our defiance to them. We are bound on a journey with these four leather-clad men, exchanging harsh glances, determined to churn through the rest of the set. Their clenched bodies indicate that they will see this night through.

'Any requests?' Wardner asks, his voice drenched in an

echo that can't be removed. In moments to come it will give his singing an almost biblical splendour.

'The Garden!' someone shouts.

Wardner nods. After a shattering cacophony of cymbals and drums a sheet metal guitar quickens the heart. *'We all wait in line,'* Wardner sings. *'A procession of no value.'*

It's as if he is delivering his last will and testament. Apt, given the vivid line from *Hamlet* apparent on his arm, *'More in sorrow than in anger'*. Even as Simon avoids certain notes, and drum links are missed, the baritone remains resolute. But the bass amp cuts out again, and the song winks into silence. 'Everything is disintegrating,' Robert says, and then the final indignity. Over the tannoy comes the information none of us were waiting for. *'Could the owner of a Red Ford Cortina please move it, as it's blocking the driveway?'*

'Give it to us!' someone shouts to our trapped protagonists. We long for Wardner to express resolve, draw his band together with a solvent glance. But the four of them remain trapped in their separate wastelands. 'Whitewashed,' Wardner announces, to angry applause.

It is to be the band's swansong. Devoid of his armoury, Jack has to play the song in half-time, slowing the song to a funereal pace. The keyboards have discovered a different language in which to speak. Each note loops back on itself, forcing keyboardist Rick Howard to create a sparse atmosphere. Simon limits himself to the few strings he has left, creating a gentle arpeggio that drives the song forward. Theo, it seems, has left one note for himself, the bass nearly mute in his arms.

Each word of Wardner's is now fully absorbed by the crowd. Poetry over a dying machine. *'You said you wanted to escape,'* he sings. *'But I never meant to bring you here.'* The song hisses and flutters. In passages it sparkles, creates an autumnal glade amongst the shattered glass. We cherish

Wardner's postcards from a distant star.

In moments like this the band have a Wagnerian splendour. Crushed by ill-luck and cursed fate they have an impact that is almost elemental. We are all transfixed by this dying sun. Wardner's words spin out amongst every tensed body. As the microphone too begins to fail, Wardner whispers his final words. We can see in his eyes that there is only one statement he wants to make, the last one we want to hear from him.

'I take full responsibility, for everything,' he says. 'You are looking at a man who's failed.'

With that, the sinking ship submerges. Wardner has gone down with it. This night is over. A night in which we are all reminded of what, at its rawest, music can be.

Salvation against all odds.

Samuel Forbes

13

Sam opened the laptop in the bedroom. With Elsa's phone seemingly still off, he felt desperate for anything to distract him. She'd never been out of contact for so long, he thought. How would she would be able to resist coming home? She had been so feverishly excited about the house. Given it was her pride and joy it had felt wrong to text her about the smashed window. Sam wondered if she was staying away to give him the chance to make the place pleasant and welcoming for her return.

Somehow, he was comforted by the familiar rubric of Google's homepage. Like a family photograph, portraying the less significant members.

Amongst the new emails there was only one relating to The National Grid. It was from a Nataly Callis.

Dear Sam. It was interesting to be able to put a face to a name. Unlike some other National Grid fans, I wanted to offer my support towards your book. Perhaps I shouldn't class myself as a fan. I think Robert would agree that I've always been more than that. I knew Robert very well during the band days. I have some information that you need. There's things that urgently need to be said before this situation escalates further. Could you come to my home in Brighton to talk? Nataly Callis

He replied in the affirmative, offering to come straight to hers. I'll pack, and then plan until Elsa calls, he thought.

Sam was surprised how many interview cassettes were gathered in the car. He emptied them from his bag, and stacked them in a neat pile on the desk. They looked shabby and adolescent, next to Elise's pristine postcards of Paris.

He took his shoes off and lay on the bed. Then closed his eyes and tried to order questions in his head.

He was awoken in the morning by the sound of the air conditioning. Throughout the night it had been working overtime, trying to warm the house given the heat leaking out of the smashed window.

He checked the phone on Elsa's pillow, hoping he had slept through a phone call. But the phone sat mute, blinking. He hated the feeling that came with having an arc of hope completed. She was in Northumberland, not Ethiopia. He wondered if he should call again. Would her phone show up all ten missed calls?

Nataly had replied in the night, offering to speak to him as soon as he could make it, and giving her address. He remembered the street she listed from his trips to indie clubs as a student. He was sure her house overlooked the sea, but somehow Sam couldn't imagine that pale, delicate woman amongst Brighton's vivid colours.

He threw his notepad, mobile and pen into a bag and made his way into the kitchen. Sunlight was blasting over the communal patio visible through the back windows.

As he poured himself a glass of orange juice, he could hear on the patio some young families making their rambunctious way onto it, enjoying the early morning sun. A young girl was being held aloft by her father, who smiled from behind designer shades. Sam was surprised to see families joining together so early in the day, but the elegant plaza had been designed to offer some communal room. It was protected by a high wall at the back of it, and Sam realized there would be few such places around. He could hear clattering from the front of the house too; no doubt he was being hemmed in on all sides by other people's happiness.

He drained the glass, before rushing outside.

But the moment he unshackled the bolt at the front of the yard he was surprised to see his car window open. He forced his bag through the gap, onto the passenger seat. It was only then that he realized the clattering at the front hadn't been a family, perhaps going down the path between the houses to the patio. The door to the neighbouring front yard had been kicked open. Sam knew he'd bolted his gate shut as he'd made his way in, but theirs had clearly looked looser. Someone had kicked it wide open, pulling off the area around the lock. The door swung ominously in the wind, exposing the still sleeping house. They have kids, Sam thought. Someone has broken in during the night.

He crept closer. He could see no sign that someone had forced entry through their front door. But if the intruder hadn't made his way into their house then that left only one alternative. They had either scaled the wall into the path, which would led only to the closed-off plaza at the back, or they had leapt over the walls between each house and got into Sam's front yard when his back was turned.

Sam rushed back to the house. The upper window to the front living room was flapping, banging in the wind with a force that Sam knew would have awoken him in the night.

Someone was in his house.

He threw his body against the front door and darted inside.

Nothing.

Sam cursed himself for leaving the phone on the upstairs bed, and his mobile in the car. Should he wedge the front door open, to have an escape route? Or trap himself inside with the intruder?

He pulled the door shut behind him. 'Who's there?' he shouted.

An instant clatter in the kitchen.

'What the hell do you want?' he shouted. He grabbed Elsa's statuette from the hallway table, and edged towards the kitchen. Sam caught a glimpse of a figure flashing across the kitchen doorway, to behind the door.

Blood pounded in his veins, all the frustration welling up. 'I'm calling the police,' he shouted. 'Get out of here now, or you'll get battered.'

His threat lacked a note of resolve. He knew it. The kitchen door slammed shut with a deafening bang. Sam gripped the statuette. Should he fight him or run? Fight or run?

The intruder made the decision for him. A roar of shattering glass filled the air. He was breaking every pane of glass in the kitchen.

The sound of children screaming filled the air. Sam could picture the families out the back, the young ones terrified. Shards thrown onto their bodies.

He dropped the statuette and ran. He slipped on the carpet, his heart in his mouth as he heard the kitchen door open. A shadow fell over Sam. The distinct shape of a man with a baseball bat.

Sam scrambled to his knees.

The front door seemed miles away. He surged towards it, footsteps pounding closer to him. He grabbed the handle, tore the door open and then pushed it behind him, against a solid human form. Sam caught a glimpse of a black boot as the body crumpled behind the door. He slammed the door shut. 'You're fucking dead, Sam,' shouted a gruff voice.

Sam ran to the car. His fingers fumbled through his pockets for the key. For a moment he forgot where the button was, smearing his fingers all over the key until it unlocked with a flash.

He glanced back. The front door began to open. Sam charged into the car, pushed the key into the ignition, and turned it. As the car squealed down the road he looked in the rear mirror, expecting to see the intruder run out. But no one was there. It was like he'd experienced a poltergeist.

As Sam pulled into a layby he thanked God that Elsa had picked up the phone this time. She had seemed almost too shocked to even agree to stay away, her voice trembling.

The policeman had been helpful. It had sounded as if he'd been eating until Sam told him that there was an intruder in his house.

'Are you in there with him?' he'd asked, the exchange slowing when Sam revealed he was speeding away in his car, to the station.

He'd been there for two hours, giving evidence in a sparse room for a DCI Beckett, a heavy-set man with rings under his eyes. Beckett constantly nodded as he wrote, before the two policewomen who'd visited the house returned and took over. One seemed more in charge, a pale woman with a set, almost plastic face and a hard set of curls. 'It looks like nothing was stolen, but some papers were spread out on the floor.'

My notes on the interviews, Sam thought.

'Probably someone chancing their arm, seeing if the new owners would be rich pickings,' Beckett said.

'Is there any reason someone would want to attack you?' he asked, before Sam described the situation. 'The National Grid,' the police officer muttered, as he scratched out notes. 'I used to like them.'

Even knowing the man had left, Sam delayed his return to the house. It greeted him with the same, hollow hum as he edged down the hallway. Except this time it had a demented edge to it.

Every glass panel in the kitchen had been smashed. The patio was deserted, plates and cups abandoned, covered with leftovers.

This is it, he thought. The end.

Sam frantically tore panels of cardboard from the box by the bin and tried to patch the windows up. When he sensed neighbours watching him he ran upstairs to check that nothing had been stolen. His shoulders dropped when he saw that his laptop, and Elsa's jewellery were still there. He circled the bedroom for a while, pushing his hand through his hair and cursing, before calling the glazier. He knew it was stupid to leave the house unsecured but he couldn't be expected to stay here now, he thought. Not with the intruder at large, and clearly after him.

14

Sam felt ridiculous driving to meet Nataly, through the drizzle and occasional bursts of violent rain, given the situation he was leaving in his wake. But she had offered answers, after all. Given how insane his life had become he was starting to grimly, determinedly, crave them.

The tall, solemn house she had given as an address looked empty. It was whitewashed, with a turret at one corner. Sam noticed through the window very few decorations in her living room as he knocked.

He heard a response inside the house, and felt himself tense.

Nataly seemed thinner than he'd remembered, the aquiline profile more pronounced in this clear ocean air. She smiled faintly in greeting, with lips the colour of dried blood. For a moment he was reluctant to go inside. The bags under the eyes and the mouth that drooped downwards even when smiling unnerved him. As he stepped over the threshold Sam saw that she was wearing an oversized white shirt, the top button done up. It faintly resembled a cassock.

'I had some trouble finding your house,' Sam started.

'I don't like to make myself too accessible.' He noticed how readily her body hunched.

The hallway was dimly lit. There was a vast print of the cover of The National Grid's album on the wall.

'Do you like it?' she asked, in a small voice.

He nodded.

'I think it's the most important thing I own. Let's sit in here,' she said.

Sam was directed into the front living room that overlooked the sea. A large white cube that reminded him of an Edward Hopper painting. There were photos on the wall, blurred shots from The National Grid's first tour. I was on that tour, he thought. But I don't remember her.

'You mentioned that you knew Robert, that you might be able to help me find him. Judging from the lack of clutter I'd presume he's not a housemate then?'

'Not any more.'

He was unable to believe how casually she made the remark. People had been speculating Wardner's every movement for years and yet she seemed so matter-of-fact. His fingers fumbled to roll the tape in his jacket pocket.

'When did you live with him? Can you shed any light on where he's been for twenty five years?'

'Yes. First, I should get you a drink.'

Nataly turned in the doorway.

'A cup of tea, please,' he said, too loud. His voice echoed with a glacial reverberation. This home isn't used to volume, Sam thought. It's used to reflection. Picking over the graveyard of the past. Turning over stones in it, which should be left to rot.

He barely had time to take in the pictures on the wall, each blurred and evocative, before she returned. She gently handed him the drink.

'He was like a mentor to me,' she said.

'Did Robert take the pictures on the wall?' he asked.

'Yes.'

'When did he give them to you?'

'He posted them to me gradually, over the course of the last twenty five years.'

'After he vanished?'

'Yes.'

'Did you see him during that time?'

'No. But they weren't all he sent me.'

'Perhaps we should begin at the start.' Sam sipped quickly as he sat in a wooden chair opposite her.

'I wrote to him as a fellow musician,' she began. 'We struck up a correspondence and he insisted on coming to see me play live.

I was in a band called Rosary.'

'You were in Rosary? I owned one of your EPs!'

She looked surprised. As she smoothed her hair he remembered the vibrant, demonstrative singer he had seen pictured in *NME*. With so much more blood and intensity than the wan, spectral vision opposite.

'I loved your record. It was so...uncompromising.'

She smiled. 'Yes. That was me. Robert came to live with me the first time he went missing. It wasn't long before he disappeared for good and even I didn't know where he was.'

'Did he explain to you why he wanted to run away?'

'No. I didn't ask then, he was too fragile. I think that he needed to get away from all distractions. The fight with his label...and one or two other parts of his life that were not going so well.'

'Did he come straight to you?'

'He phoned not long after he went missing. He had been travelling by train. Asked if he could stay.'

'It was November when he went missing. So around then?'

'Yes. Winter.'

This is amazing, Sam thought, sitting up. A big piece of the jigsaw has fallen into place. 'So was he with you for long?'

'A few months. I tried to keep him there, safe, but after a while he left.'

Sam blew at his tea.

'What did he do for that whole time?'

'Very little. At first he was like a damaged bird. I'd built up this private little world in which I'd begun to create, and until then he'd helped me. Given me confidence. But when he moved in it was payback time. I had to drop everything. My work, my art, just to keep him alive. How to get him to change his clothes, eat his meals. I went from barely knowing this guy, idolising him, to practically changing his nappy. Whilst getting better, he took and he took and he took. I didn't realise how much he'd taken from me until he left. The intensity of that time, and the way he deserted me after I'd nourished him…it was overpowering. I was spent after that. I found it hard to get back on my feet. Very hard.'

'I keep wondering…why did you do so much for him?'

'Times when I was teetering, he pulled me back. I had to give him refuge.'

'So why have you kept this quiet? Fear of your relationship being misinterpreted?'

'No. People could not have understood it anyway. We didn't have a traditional boyfriend-girlfriend relationship, but it was close. He had been teaching me to mine my own inner world, and to be disciplined about it. To create bizarre rituals that allow it to make sense to me.'

She leant back, a triangle of dark hair falling over one eye. She left it there, pursing her pale lips.

'You said there were things that urgently needed to be said?'

'Yes. It was Bonny who first put me in touch with him. When Robert revealed to her that he was alive, after so many years, he must have mentioned that I had taken him in, as he needed some space from his wife. Bonny was apparently angry with me. Furious that I had harboured him after all she had done to put him on the map. But it wasn't only him that had become well-known. I was starting to become known as an artist myself; but after Robert went, I had to drop all that. Seeing how unhinged he was, how far he had come undone, left a mark. I left my job, my home, and ran away to the coast. People had seen the two of us getting closer and closer and so they assumed I'd vanished too.'

'So with you and Robert going missing at the same time, people wondered if…'

She nodded. 'Word started to spread that he had been taken in by an over-zealous fan who asked too much of him. Rumours built that he had eventually driven her down to the sea and…'

'Murdered her.'

Guy Mankowski

'It was Bonny who distorted the truth. Robert was always scared of how brilliantly manipulative she could be. I think in her mind Bonny thought, 'Robert has abandoned me. But if people think he is guilty of even more than that, I will be getting my own back'.'

'I see.'

'And by casting me as the obsessive fan, she also gave me a neat little kick in the teeth too.'

'How do you know she did that?'

'At the gallery, in London. At the end of the night, she couldn't resist taking me to one side and boasting about what she'd done. Said it would make the band's comeback the biggest in history. Kept going on about how it would secure her fame, as an artist, and finally be payback for all the investment Robert took from her.'

'Jesus.'

'There's more. Let me show you something, Sam. It's the correspondence I've received from Robert since he disappeared. I've never shown it to anyone.'

She went out, and returned with a sheaf of postcards.

'I believe these shed light on where he is now. They offer answers on where he has been, for all these years.'

Sam took them reverently.

'But the puzzle only fits together for me, as I sent him the postcards which provoked these responses. So only I hold all the pieces.'

'Why do you want to help me?'

'I know a lot of the fans are saying that if he wants to stay missing, you should respect that. I have heard about them giving you a hard time.'

'You don't know the half of it.'

'Exactly. If the mystery isn't solved soon, these rumours will continue to build and someone is going to get badly hurt.'

'So you say Robert started sending these after he disappeared?'

She nodded. 'The first came through at the end of 1981, when no one had any idea where he was.'

He looked up at her. 'And you didn't want to share it with his family? Or his wife?'

Her expression tightened. The colour fell from her face. 'Certainly not. Robert and I had a relationship deeper than anyone could understand. Because I was there for him when things went wrong.' She lifted her chin defiantly. 'Francesca wasn't.'

Sam began to flick through them.

'They came once every few years,'

The first was a postcard of what appeared to be a field. On the back, in Robert's distinct scrawl, were the words 'I hope you are still writing. Take care, R.'

The 'g', Sam noted, was looped. Just like on the postcards online.

'This field could be anywhere,' Sam said.

'I know. But it's the next one that got me thinking.'

'But how do you know these are from Robert?'

'These postcards are the reason I haven't moved from here in twenty-five years. He set me a mission he wanted me to see through. I can't leave until he's found.'

'You could have had the post redirected?'

'What if he needed me again?'

'It is one hell of a sacrifice.'

'You don't understand, Sam. Robert saved my life. I was going mad until he came along.'

'But you said yourself, he took you to the brink.'

'Perhaps loyalty can sometimes be misplaced.'

The second postcard was of what looked like a white stone, French or perhaps Belgian hotel. It was simply signed, 'Love, R.' In the third postcard, a whitewashed building with pillars was set back from a courtyard and in faint pencil Sam could see one window of it had been circled. Sam looked on the back of them.

The postmarks on the first few were too blurred to read, but the last ones were clearly marked 'Antwerp.'

'1987, that one. They show where he was staying at the time.'

'It doesn't mention anything about you keeping them to yourself though,' Sam said.

'At that point they were too vague to warrant a journey. I spoke to people who know Antwerp, and both said this hotel looked more seaside than city. Ostend was mentioned at one point, particularly with regards to the next few.'

Sam flicked through a few postcards of European street scenes.

'My guess was that he had sent me the postcards so I knew he was okay, as he was passing through. By the time I'd worked out where he was, he'd have moved. I'd always be behind. The press were dying to know where he was, but for the wrong reasons. If he was moving I figured he obviously didn't want to be found yet. But he wanted the people he was closest to to know he was alive.'

But not his wife? Sam didn't feel bold enough to ask the question.

The next one, though cut to be the same shape as a postcard, was a photo. It depicted a country scene, with wet grass and trees, but this time somewhere very English-looking. In the background of the photo, slightly out of focus, Sam could just about make out a range of hills.

'This one was sent very recently. Look at the note on the back,' Nataly implored.

"Everyone must come out of exile in their own way,' Martin Buber,' Sam read.

'One of his favourite philosophers. I remember he once talked about him. You see, in that note Robert is telling me that he's deciding to come out of hiding. And look at the last one,' Nataly continued, leaning further in. Her neck bones threatened to burst through her shirt.

Sam looked at the picture of the last postcard. It was a shot of what seemed the base of a series of hills, and in one corner of it was a small, white building. 'And the quote,' Nataly said.

Sam read the words out loud. '*NATALY. I COULD NEVER BE FAR FROM MANCHESTER, NOT FOR LONG.*' Then, in a clumsy attempt at italics, was written, '*Come live with me and be my love / And we will all the pleasures prove / That valleys, groves, hills, and fields / Woods or steepy mountain yields.*'

'Marlowe was one of his favourite playwrights,' she said. 'You see? The last postcard is the final clue. He's asking me to find him. The last two are clearly somewhere in Northern England, out in the country. He talks of mountains, and opens with the statement that he could never be far from Manchester. And what mountain range starts in Greater Manchester?'

'I don't know. The Pennines?' Sam said.

'The Pennines,' Nataly echoed, with a smile. 'That's the second to last time I've heard from him.'

'And the last?'

'A phone call. Late at night, not long ago at all. I was in such a deep sleep I almost thought it was a dream.'

'You're sure it was him?'

'Yes. I asked where he was. He said 'I've finally found my home. I'm staying in a monastery'.'

'Somewhere in the Pennine region.'

'If one exists.'

And if you're not a fantasist, Sam thought. He was unable to take his eyes off the postcards. So many answers, tied up on those tattered pieces of paper. Answers he had given so much to hear. Yet the links between them seemed too disparate to be credible.

'If he wants you to find him,' Sam asked 'why doesn't he just tell you that directly?'

'He isn't that straightforward a person. I sometimes wonder if he is even aware of the direction he pulls people in. He seems to need to test people. Get them to prove their devotion to him, for some reason.'

'I have got a sense of that.'

'I hope you don't find this too strange but...I would rather keep hold of these cards,' she said.

'No, of course. I understand.'

Suddenly, she clutched the side of her stomach.

'Are you okay?' Sam asked.

'It's fine, it's only cramp. It's since that damn operation.'

'Can I get you anything?'

'I just need to take something,' she said, wincing. 'I won't be a moment.'

As soon as she had left the room Sam pulled his phone out of his bag and, listening carefully for the sound of her movements, shakily started to take pictures of the other cards.

He cursed himself for his unsteady hand and was trying to position the camera for more focused shots of the final postcards when he heard Nataly returning.

She came in, still wincing.

'Do you feel any better?' he asked.

She nodded, and reached out for the pictures.

'Well, what do you think?' she smiled weakly.

'I think you're right. He is leading you to him.'

'I know. There's no way I can go to him, not in this state. You don't need to, but at least you can use your book to put these rumours to bed. Answer the questions about where he is and where he's been. It would be enough to settle all this agitation.'

'Sure. But if I'm honest, I don't think that would be enough for me,' Sam said.

'Sam,' she answered. 'Just because he didn't kill me, doesn't mean he doesn't have something to hide.'

'What do you mean?'

She shifted, fingering the corner of a photo.

'When I spoke to him I didn't know that Bonny was behind those rumours. I asked him, 'Why don't you come back? Why don't you resume your life?' He told me he couldn't. He has a lot of guilt. He thinks he's a murderer.'

'Are you sure he was being literal?'

'Yes. It's a big part of why he's stayed hidden.'

Sam had the same feeling as when someone had broken into his house. That same low, chilling buzz. 'Who did he kill?'

'He wouldn't tell me. He said he didn't want to drag me into his darkness any more.'

Sam wiped the sweat from his brow. 'I suppose that would be the real answer to the mystery,' he said.

'But it also means that he isn't safe to go after, Sam. Leave him where he is. There is a reason he has gone to the monastery. He seeks absolution, from whatever he did. He clearly does not want anyone but me going after him.'

'My commission was to find him, to get the story from him. Anything less feels like a failure.'

She shook her head, her mouth twisting for a second as if she was holding back tears. 'It's not worth the risk.'

ROBERT WARDNER

Tottenham Court Road is the start of the apocalypse. I'm on the escalator on the way up, hugging myself. Last night gargoyles came out of the woodwork and they cackled and spat. They swirled in my room. You look at them and they dissolve in the dark. I couldn't work out where the mirror ended and the chair began and you think about it until they become a new person.

I need something to eat. I need to find a decent changing room to wash in. Remember how important your appearance used to be? Back then you'd have never shaved your head if your hair was getting at you. You'd only cut yourself in places that the camera wouldn't find. You'd have never got up, pulled on a parka, prised yourself out into the world. If you'd had a night with the gargoyles you'd have slept it off. In the morning made a list of what to do, to fix yourself.

You know what happens when you just keep going, Robert. You run yourself into the ground. Your body breaks when it hits concrete. Flesh is not as hard as metal and stone.

I push through the gate of the tube station, for the street. What exit do I want?

A guard is tapping his fat fingers on the turnstile. He knows I've got no ticket. He's going to throw me in prison. I'll have to fight him.

Move over to the newsagent. If I buy something, maybe he'll let me go. It'll show I can contribute to society. I fish for dirty silver. When I turn around he's gone. Gone to get another security guard. I run. Run run running.

On the street outside all hands are outstretched. Trying to take my money or give me papers. It's like being shoved into a dirty, hissing wind tunnel. I want to know what his agenda is, and his and his and his and his. Everyone's hurrying, it must be for somewhere. They've all been set an assignment I'm kept out of. Why else would they be this focused?

Capitalism throbs like a vein. About to burst. It nags everyone to move, over each other, trample each other down. I don't dare turn. The man in the grey coat is always at the bottom of every set of stairs. Run raw.

Where can I find out the plan? Can he tell me?

I remember. I did have a plan.

I push past the elbows and handbags. Towards Soho. There are stalls and strips all around, but they will soon fade back into the ether. Right now they're stuck onto the shiny surfaces, but soon they'll be prised off. In the cleansing flood.

Everything here is temporary, everything is dirty. Everywhere has been used, violated, covered in fluid.

I am. Missing. The. Part. Of. Me. That. Pretends. There. Is. Not. Too. Much. Dirt.

Before, I was like everyone else. I pushed through the filth. Now I can see it all around, making fingertips stick to every surface. People walk, with other people's fluid in their mouths and stomachs and wombs, other people's dirt on their fingers and lips. Playing round the corner of their mouth. The dank sweat of their hair and the dried, rank sweat of the past.

I've lost the ability to pretend it's not there, and now the dirty tide spins into my ears. It's drowning me.

I push down the street.

It's not just the physical world that's filthy. Language corrupts, coerces. The thoughts of a ruling class filter onto subservient creatures, coaxing them into apathy. Adverts sedate, seduce, arouse, pacify.

There is no agenda, I tell myself. It's the motion you want to look at. It's this forward, impatient moment that is life. All the elbows and fabrics and answers swimming past you. You'll only find the answer by joining the shoal.

Like everything else, food here is hot and immediate. You can eat pieces of meat, different shades of brown, that fall off a silver stick. A stick that spins like a model on a catwalk.

Who told you to put this in your body? Who decided that this is alright? When you look at it sat in that plastic it's like the twenty-first *century's final, grotesque insult.*

I twist downstream, down the dirty canal. A carrier bag on the filthy surface. Flowing towards an unknown destination. I could get caught on a rock and flap there for years. Who is watching out for me, to prise me off?

No one is.

Look for a pub, a place that I can stop and make myself clean. A place I can drink myself right.

I pass a Chinese restaurant, in the window a rack of ducks' tongues. The display crammed with brown shining carcasses, rotating slowly. Like Victorian corpses, hung by the bridge.

Knife left. Take a short cut down a small alleyway. Something compels me down it. I don't know what it is. There's an art gallery. One of the centre-pieces is a painted version of our album cover.

I must have lost it, if I think I can see that.

The paint inside each of the six grids speaks to me. Babbles with incoherent tongues. They have been injected with the artist's pain.

They set it up in the window so I would pass by and see my reflection in it. So I would stop trying to work them out.

Must get out of the city.

Reel back onto the street. Find my way back to the road with the ducks' tongues.

If only they knew how sorry I was. But repentance is just more pain.

I remember my motto when I first came here, when I was on the twenties tightrope. An internal motto I used to say to myself. To make myself focus.

'I am so fucked'.

In toilets, looking down at the limp jet of urine, wallowing in the loyal smell of my own shit. Pale-faced in the mirror, looking like wreckage. Preparing for some absurd meeting I didn't believe in. A photo shoot, an interview with a dead soul, a bright-eyed fanzine girl. Wanting to use my debris to build her own raft.

I knew then that I didn't fit. I knew even then that I was only a blip on the landscape, that the weather would change. The attempts to make me marketable would end. Attempts to hide my spots, shrink my belly, shield my past. There were only a few pieces of something unique inside me and the publicity machines didn't know what it was or how to use it.

There were moments of cleanliness, when I was young,

Perfume on Frankie's arms as she lay on the grass in Durham. Yes, it made sense there. In that city.

Frankie would have gripped my hand, and calmed my nerves on the tube. Frankie would have assured me no one was looking. Frankie would have taken me to her favourite Chinese restaurant off Tottenham Court Road. The one with the ducks tongues in the window.

We'd have had Peking duck. I'd have felt her strength. It would make me want to fight on.

To our last recording session.

To where we left off.

I'd reclaim the moment. Meet Simon, for a pint, somewhere in the city. Become focused enough to go back into the studio.

Get those songs back.

But I can't, not now. I've torn it. I took it too far.

I need her. I need to feel clean again. I need to feel purified.

That's where I've got to go.

15

As he approached the front door, Sam felt his muscles harden. Did he need to grab a weapon?

Elsa had left just one message to say she was going home but since then, nothing. What if the intruder had tied her up and killed her? He realised he was running on empty. A car freewheeling down the hill, with the brake-lines cut.

The house seemed dead, like a show-home after hours. Edging down the hallway Sam could see a light in the kitchen.

'Elsa?' he called.

'I'm in here.'

In the muted light Elsa was ladling soup into containers, dripping it over the counter. Behind her the windows were covered in cardboard. As she turned to greet Sam, Elsa was ashen-faced.

'Look at our house,' she said. For a moment she broke down. 'This is our home.'

Sam put his knapsack on the counter top, unnerved by the bloodless feel of her body.

'Jesus.'

'What did they want? I've looked around, nothing's been taken, Sam.'

'They wanted to scare me off the book.'

'Please, please tell me they have?'

Sam looked at the shattered panes of glass. 'If that's what you want.'

Elsa couldn't bring herself to nod. As she looked up at Sam she had an expression he hadn't seen before. It was more than resignation, but he couldn't be sure.

'I was hoping you would be home, Elsa. It feels like we haven't seen each other in ages.'

'I know.'

Elsa moved between the work surface and the fridge, moving the boxes around with tired precision. Sam wondered if he noticed a slight tremor in her hand.

'I feel terrible for leaving the gallery opening the way I did. It looked as if it was going so well.' He moved clumsily onto a kitchen stool, tried to read her muffled body language.

He waited for her to turn, to respond. She didn't. 'But it wasn't a waste of time. I've been told where Wardner is.'

She smiled, weakly. 'At least all this led to something, then.'

'It's not enough to get the money. On my way back I had a call from the publisher. He said that the public opinion is turning against Mason House. My book is being given as the reason why the band's tour dates have been postponed. Martin told me that unless I speak to Wardner in the next day or so, he's pulling the plug.'

'You must be joking. We have to try and fix our home, Sam. Before one of us gets killed.'

'I know. I am so close to finding him, though.'

He wanted to take her shoulders, but sensed somehow she would shrug him off.

'There's a message for you on the answer phone, Sam.'

His papers were still spread on the floor. He thought of alien hands rifling through them and shuddered.

He clicked the answerphone on. There was a long pause and then a voice growled. Low and steady.

'This is Patrick Wardner. I am Robert Wardner's cousin and I…we.' He seemed to be addressing someone else in the room with him. 'We want to talk to you.'

There was something about the voice. He could imagine the owner of it smashing windows. Had he heard it before?

Patrick's brusque message ended with his number. Sam scrawled it onto on a scrap of paper.

Elsa lingered in the doorway. As Sam turned she handed him

a mug of coffee.

'Sound promising?'

'I will call him back later. I know we have more pressing concerns.'

'It's okay,' she replied. 'You can call him now if you think he can help you.'

'No. I don't think he can, somehow.'

The man at the other end picked up on the first ring, and grunted his name.

'Mr Wardner, it's Samuel Forbes.'

'And you're the hack writing about my cousin?' He had the same, thick Mancunian accent as Robert. For a second Sam wondered if in fact it was him.

He moved over to the living room window. Outside two young children stood over a bike, deciding who should mount it first.

'Ex-hack. Now author.'

'So are you the man hunting Robert or are you telling me I've made a mistake?'

Sam could feel blood swell in his temple.

'I am a huge admirer of your cousin's work. I was the journalist who wrote about their first gigs, who brought them to a lot of people's attention.'

'You brought him attention? Well, what do we owe you?'

'I am passionate about writing this book because I want more people to appreciate Robert's work. I know this book is controversial,' he continued. 'But I really didn't want to upset anyone.'

'So it's a labour of love, is it?'

The voice sounded as if it had toiled through years of cigarette smoke.

Sam hunched forward. 'Absolutely.'

'So you're not getting a fee?'

'Patrick...'

'Mr Wardner. Let's not get ahead of ourselves.'

This isn't our first stand-off, Sam thought. We had one through the kitchen door.

'I apologise. I have had hate mail, bricks thrown through my window and the other day we were broken into. I am being paid a pittance for this.'

'So you need to find my cousin to get paid?' The voice rose. 'I think I get it.'

Sam went to speak, but stopped himself. 'I want to speak to your cousin, Mr Wardner, to make this book as good as it can possibly be.'

'Better for him, or for you?'

'Both.'

'But he won't be seeing any money from it, will he? It won't help him with his treatment and that?'

'Mr Wardner, I'm not sure why you first rang me.'

He felt his temper rising.

The question seemed to outflank Patrick.

'I'm just giving you a call to see what you're after.'

How did he have his number? Sam certainly hadn't sent him an email. In his mind, family members had always been out of bounds.

'Ok,' Sam said. 'Perhaps we need to meet face-to-face. Would you be prepared to answer a couple of questions about your cousin?'

'I don't know him that well. But I know when a family member of mine gets in the papers all right. To step in if someone wants to cause him pain, when he's already been through enough for one lifetime.'

'Does Robert feel harassed?'

'Someone starts calling your exes. Sniffing around your past. Wouldn't you feel like you was getting run into the ground?'

'I don't know. Not if the book was being approached sensitively.'

'He's trying to ease himself back into his life, his family. People putting pressure on him now could make him crack, and we'd lose him forever. You got any idea what a hole he left in our lives when he vanished?'

'Of course not...'

'We're not going to let you finish him off just so you can see your name in lights. You need to try putting yourself in someone else's shoes,' Patrick continued. 'I doubt if you've ever felt hemmed in. To the point where you want to leave it all behind.'

'You're wrong. I feel that way now.'

Patrick, surprised by the remark, seemed to sigh. 'You do?'

'I can promise you, Mr Wardner. I don't want to do anything to hurt him. As a family member, you were there in the early days weren't you? You saw how hard it was for him to get noticed, over all those London types? To teach himself, note by note, to write songs. After all that, doesn't he deserve to have people finally pay attention to his work, while he's still around?'

'I don't know you, son, and I don't know how long you've been around for. But I do know when I'm being played. It might work on your college mates but it won't wash with a man of the world.'

'I was hoping you might be able to put me in touch with him.'

Silence.

'I spoke to someone. Someone who thought he might be in a monastery,' Sam said.

Still no response.

'I'd be interested to hear if you think that might be the case?'

'No. Robert is not up there.'

Up there? That seems to suggest north of here. Yet I never mentioned The Pennines, Sam thought.

'Okay.' Sam tried to sound disconsolate, but suspected he hadn't managed it. I'm onto something here, he thought.

'I've got to go,' Patrick said. 'But Sam?'

'Yes, Mr Wardner?'

'I hope your house gets sorted soon.'

There was a few moments of silence before Sam acknowledged that he had rung off.

ROBERT WARDNER

There's a cloud of smoke building over the drum risers.

It happens, that. The music takes everything out of your body. Out of everyone's body. It all merges into a cloud that hangs over us.

Jack bangs out a slow, trembling beat with one hand. For a moment I don't know if the song has started, but then I recognise it. It's in my DNA. As I turn towards my men I see a faint map of the song already. I know its slow moments. Its tender moments. The moments I can miss and the moments I must grip. It's a song I've sung when I'm half-alive and a song I'll sing when I'm gone. I just know.

I look up. In this golden light the members of the audience have altered. They have each shed their flesh. They're no longer living entities now, just these distant silhouettes. They altered like a melody shifting key. We have all slipped into another realm. Rick starts this tremulous keyboard line over that aching beat. There is room enough between each note to live and die.

Right now, gripping this dying microphone, I know it is my job to commune with these people. To guide them into another realm. I shake my head and remember to sing. Words that are now carved into my bones.

As I open my dry mouth it's as if I'm remembering words from a sacred scroll. We respond to the moans and urges of the mind and flesh as if they're ours alone, but they belong to all of us.

I recount those words for their benefit. To guide those waiting silhouettes towards their horizon.

Every silhouette has got this aura around it now. On some people the aura is white, like spun gold, and just floats out from them. Sometimes it tries, cautiously, to merge with other auras. In one or two cases it eases out and combines with another. Forms this shared light.

Mostly they just quiver, sadly, by themselves.

Behind all of them is a row of darker silhouettes. As I sing, slower now, I squint to see if they are really stooping. These dark ones are waiting for me to fall, once my duty is complete. Then, I know, they will sweep my bones away. They are still. Their battles have been won and lost a long time ago.

The silhouettes closer to me wait, as precious moments in the verse pass like wasted days. They do not yet know that I have been sent to sing them private messages of salvation. I have to convince them to hear my song, and once they have, they look up to me as if I am the light.

But the silhouettes behind know my purpose all too well. Once it is done, they will take the light out of me, and then take my body away with them.

16

After letting the glazier into the house, Sam moved into the bedroom and collapsed on the sheets. He tried to piece it all together in his mind. The Marlowe quote. Manchester, The Pennines. A monastery.

He engaged the laptop. At first the digital world, nonplussed by his sudden determination, resisted. He searched using various combinations of the key terms and, to his relief, the pieces quickly came together.

Milfield Monastery. The only sheltered monastic community in The Pennine region. An Anglican community which, according to an article about their vineyard, offered individuals respite from the world and the chance to devote their lives to God.

The monastery's website suggested that anyone interested stay at first for a few days to become familiar with the austerity of a monk's life. See if they would fit in with the discipline of a life in silence, living with few amenities, and working with other monks. Sam found it hard to believe that the cravenly ambitious singer, who sometimes violently clashed with those around him, could tolerate that calm lifestyle. He would have to however, in order to become a novitiate, on the route to becoming a fully-fledged monk. If all this sounded outlandish, one phrase did catch Sam's attention. 'A monk must abandon home and culture in a profound sense,' it said. If he was hiding in the monastery, Wardner would have had to have stepped out of The National Grid for good.

With his last embers of energy Sam took down details. Amongst the pile of books they had never shelved was an atlas, and with a blunt crayon he sketched a quick route on the crisp page. The train would be quicker, he realized.

Whilst Sam frantically searched online, the glazier and his assistant brought large panes of glass into the house. During the two hours that Elsa watched them restore their home her sense of self-loathing began to shrink. In its place there was now burgeoning warmth, almost a melancholy.

It drove her to light small tea-lights around the house, scent the air, and put flowers in the living room. Her desire to build a nest for Sam surprised her. He's upstairs, she thought, about to complete his life's work. Perhaps Wardner can't harm us, because he's too old. Perhaps once Sam finds him we'll be left alone by whoever did this. Perhaps we can get the life we planned for.

As Sam came downstairs, Elsa felt buoyed by his reaction to her work. The dimmed lights, the lounge-rock on the stereo. He appeared touched by the sandwich she offered as she sat on the sofa opposite. As she settled back into the chair she tracked the way his hands searched for warmth in the toasted bread.

'You came down sooner than I thought you would,' she said.

'I just had to find out if this monastery existed. But now I know, I thought we should talk. I know we're long overdue a chat.' He put the sandwich down and moved his chair closer to her.

As his eyes traced around her cheekbones Elsa wished she'd spent more time trying to look desirable. What had happened to the girl with the glitter and the journal?

'I hope you know,' he continued, 'that I only stuck with this book because I wanted to make a success of myself. So that I didn't let you down again.'

Elsa felt like she'd been whipped. When she looked she felt her eyes wetten. 'It just looked to me like it was the same old Sam.'

'Well, it wasn't. You said at the start you were worried where this book would take me. Now I can see what you meant.'

'Sam.'

She closed her eyes, and for a moment took in the atmosphere.

The scented candles, the soft mood. Why had she created the very setting she longed for, on the day she would destroy it all?

'What is it? Something's on your mind.'

'Yes. It is.'

'Are you going to tell me?'

'Yes. On the night of the launch, Sam, I did something terrible.'

'What?'

She looked at her hands.

'What did you do?'

'I...slept with Malcolm.'

Sam watched the words come out of her mouth. He traced the sound it made in the room. The way it reverberated on the walls. But it was only when her lips closed, after she said it, that he believed what he had heard. 'You slept with him?'

She winced.

'You couldn't have done,' he said. 'He's an old man. A relic. You know how much I hate him, how much I've suspected he's after you. And I've been doing all this for you!'

She looked up at the ceiling, and felt a hot tear burn its way down her cheek.

'I made a mistake,' she said.

'Why?'

His voice shook the walls.

'I was angry at you. I thought you were off on a stupid mission to get yourself killed. I couldn't take it much more.'

'Jesus Christ!'

'I thought you weren't there for me!'

'And he is? You think he really cares about you?'

She flapped her hands. 'No. I know now that he doesn't.'

'Now? After he got what he wanted from you?'

She shook her head.

'Look around you, Sam. We've got the home we wanted. Finally, we've made a home for ourselves. Let's not blow it now, eh? What is it you always say? That this time next year, Rodders, we'll be millionaires?'

He shook his head.

Her voice dropped. She leant in, put her hand on his. 'We can make a clean slate.'

Sam looked up, his eyes boiling. 'Do you want to know something?'

'What?' she whispered.

'When I first came back from London after that meeting I thought of the Elsa I first met. You remember? When I was ill she was there, no matter what. I thought of the life she deserved to have.'

'Oh, Sam.'

'And it was that thought that pushed me out to meet all those freaks.'

'I know, Sam.'

'When did you sleep with him?'

'The night you went off with Bonny.'

He stood up. Suddenly all the words, the interviews, fell away like demolished houses. Shattered by a wrecking ball. 'You can't have slept with him.'

'I'll leave my job. We can find a way out of this!'

Sam looked at her; the way her eyes narrowed as she pleaded.

He thought of the girl in their halls of residence. Who sat on the end of her bed clutching her journal. With the blueprint to his future concealed within it.

As he walked up the stairs Sam felt winded. He heard Elsa move in the kitchen, and she didn't come after him.

He walked into the bathroom, locked the door, and sat down on the floor. There were certain flashes of the past that snagged him, that made him unable to stand. As they reverberated in his mind the tears came easily. He was surprised at how much the small white bathroom shook when they began to flood out of him.

He wasn't sure if the feeling would last. This wrenching pain in his abdomen. He knew it wouldn't subside for as long as he stayed within these walls.

17

As he left the train at Milfield, Sam couldn't help thinking of the dinner he'd had with Elsa when they first moved in. 'You're walking into your own grave,' she'd said.

The station itself seemed a throwback to the very era Sam associated with Wardner. Perspex tunnels over each platform, fogged with time. The harsh, red steel finishing, so evocative of eighties' industry. Even if Sam felt the journey was absurd, Milfield was straight out of the singer's palette.

The rain was still waiting to fall as the monastery loomed into view. It was not the bleak, end of the road spectacle Sam had anticipated. At the entrance, to his right, men busied themselves with the construction of a wedding marquee. Ahead of him, at the tip of a lush green lawn, was an elegant, green-domed building. Behind it sat the rugged profile of the Pennines.

Sam cursed himself for not having brought a full map. He would just have to search for the hut, using the photo as a guide.

As he approached the dome, something caught his attention. To the right of the sandstone building was a cluster of small wooden huts. Something about them reminded him of Nataly's picture. He had it on his phone. He held the image up against the backdrop. That was it. That same curve of hills, dipping like a cello on its side. So, if the dip was there, he thought, the white hut should be just to the right of it.

A figure was approaching him. A monk in a black robe. But Sam felt too close to his prize to give up now. With a sudden spurt of energy he made his way to the side of the building and rounded it. He came up against a stone white wall. He reeled back in shock, his foot plunging into a hidden pocket of soft mud. He checked the picture again, scarcely able to believe it. This was the hut.

He had found it. Wardner, he thought, has recently been here.

Pushing the thought of the advancing man from his mind, Sam tracked backwards. It looked as if the photo had been taken about twenty feet from the hut. Which would mean Wardner had been standing right up against the perimeter fence.

Sam surged, determined to see the small hut from the very place at which Wardner had stood. Seconds later he was there, leant against the barbed-wire fence. Holding up the picture next to the white building.

It was a perfect match.

The wind whipped around him in congratulation.

'Excuse me.'

The monk was approaching the hut, his head stooped into the wind as he ran. 'You can't trespass here,' he shouted, 'This is a private retreat. You have to leave, now.'

The rain began to come down as Sam stepped forward, into more mud. 'I didn't realize,' he said. 'I'm sorry.'

'You can't just wander around here,' the monk shouted, covering his eyes from the gust. 'What do you want?'

'I need to speak to someone,' Sam said. Thunder cracked overhead and the rain streaked his face. 'I have to speak to someone,' he repeated, loudly, over the wailing wind.

Once the heat of the prior's study had warmed him, Sam stood up and walked over to the fire. He sensed the prior's stare behind him.

'You were close to the most sacred part of our establishment,' the prior said, his voice low. 'There are so few places now in which a person can immerse themselves in their studies of the Bible. At Milfield we pride ourselves on having created a holy site. Where one can devote themselves to God, unimpeded.'

'I understand,' Sam said, without turning.

'And we take the privacy of our guests very seriously indeed. I could never violate that sanctum, no matter how important this book of yours is.'

As Sam turned to face him in the spacious office the prior coughed, shuffling in his seat behind his desk. His white hair glowed in the firelight.

There is nothing for it, Sam thought. I have to be honest.

'Please accept my apology. I have not come into this site respectfully. The truth is, I am unravelling.'

The moment he said the words something inside him give way.

I am no longer pretending to be a professional, a serious investigator, he thought. I drop all my pretences.

He met the prior's eye. He could smell the rain drying on his clothes. Beyond the old windows surrounding them, the storm raged. The prior held his gaze, the lines on his forehead quivering, as he weaved his fingers together.

'I am not here to try and make money,' Sam continued. 'In fact, I've never made money out of anything.' He looked down for a moment. 'I've made nothing of my life. Everything I have done has failed.'

The prior exhaled.

'I've never known how it feels to see something through. This man's music meant the world to me. I've been trying to track him down not for fame or glory, but to prove something to myself. To prove that I can accomplish something.'

The prior bowed his head.

Sam stepped forward. 'I've sacrificed so much for this. My girlfriend has left me for another man. I've lost my home. Been hounded. But now I've arrived at the place where I know he's staying.'

He could read nothing from the expression of the prior.

'I don't want to damage the sanctity of your monastery... I just need to feel like I have finally reached my goal.'

The prior looked at the fire. His brow furrowed. Sam could only read in his expression a precise kind of resignation.

'I am sorry,' he said. 'But I cannot help you. I simply cannot comment on who takes refuge with us.'

He pushed back in his chair, moved around the desk and over to Sam. He placed his hand on his shoulder.

Sam lowered his head. Something inside him shifted. To his surprise, a hot tear spiralled down his face and onto his coat.

'I do not in all truth believe that finding this man will take you to the end,' the prior said. 'I am afraid you have a more fundamental, spiritual malady Sam. You have been seeking answers in the wrong place.'

His hand lifted. 'Perhaps though, I can assist you with that.'

Sam didn't reply.

'You said you have booked a seat on the eleven o' clock train tomorrow. We are not an inhospitable bunch here at Milfield, Sam. You have come to see us and you won't return completely unsatisfied. Tomorrow morning, come to my cottage in the valley for breakfast at nine. I will show you around the grounds. I'll see if I can assist with what I think truly troubles your heart.'

Slowly, Sam nodded. 'The grounds?' he said. 'I saw on the website. Isn't there a graveyard?'

'You will find your answer,' he said. 'Just not on the terms by which you seek it.'

18

The room in the hotel was small but quiet. Sam turned the TV on but was unable to now concetrate. All the dazzling sensations and images repulsed him.

He turned the volume down and tore into the contents of the mini-bar. He could not remember going to sleep, but when he awoke in the morning he was surrounded by small, empty bottles. The jolt of pain in his head indicated that he had probably slept for too long to catch his train.

What was I going back to anyway, he wondered?

The acid sense of disappointment trickled into his consciousness, like violence, remembered from television images. Focusing on the clock by the bed he was surprised to see it was only 8.02. He had never taken the prior's offer of breakfast seriously but amidst the mental fog of morning it suddenly occurred to him. He could still make it.

The Prior had asked Sam to knock, at nine, on the red-doored cottage at the foot of the valley. But this morning the cottages weren't even visible. Although each blade of grass underfoot looked pin-sharp, the horizon was an impenetrable bar of silver mist. It concealed his destination, and was softened only by the sunlight that illuminated its slender margins.

Sam felt as if he was walking into another realm, moving into that mysterious haze which kept its contents hidden. In the distance, now only just visible through the fog, were a couple of partially thatched cottages. He assumed one of them was the prior's.

It was a small, modest affair just off the mud track. A tiny worn path revealed the way there. It sat in the crook where the valley swiftly became high hills. Though from a distance the cottage looked unkempt, abandoned even, Sam saw that up close it had a well-loved air.

Sam passed the first two houses, both seemingly deserted. Instead of a front garden they had small, well-kept graveyards. He found the red door to be ajar, and the prior welcomed him inside with a keen shout of his name.

Sam found himself on a small, frayed patch of carpet in front of a roaring fire, a kettle singing in the kitchen. Through the back windows, against the sudden hills, gardeners were beginning work on what appeared to be a chaotic allotment. They moved in and out of each other, rakes and spades slung over broad shoulders. The prior gestured for Sam to make himself comfortable at a table holding piles of books.

'I am so pleased you decided to see me before going, Sam,' he said, with open arms.

He was not dressed in a robe, but in a tattered blue overall. 'I must admit, I still feel rather guilty about the hostile reception you received when you first came here. I blame it on enthusiastic young members of our brethren.'

'Please don't,' Sam said. 'I feel so embarrassed by my little speech.'

The prior stood over him for a moment, before admiring the fog through the back window. 'Not desperate Sam, driven. Determined.' He clenched his fist with a small smile. 'Sheer gumption. God put that inside your heart for a reason, Sam. Allow it to guide you.'

Sam tried to smile.

'The coffee will be ready in a moment. Tell me, Sam, are you a man of faith?'

The sound of the bristling fire eased his nausea. He considered it, as the kettle whistled itself to the boil. The prior moved into the kitchen to pour, the white wisps of hair above his ears lit for a moment by sudden sunlight through the windows. As he returned Sam saw that his hands were worn and slightly scarred, as if they had given themselves over to the earth long ago.

'I used to have faith, certainly.'

Sam received the mug and took a sip.

'Used to? And yet yesterday, you seemed surprised by your own desperation.'

The coffee warmed Sam's lips, smoothed out the pain in his temple. The prior moved in front of him, blocking the glow. 'Forgive me. We don't get the chance to converse with too many outsiders. But your quest intrigued me.'

'You think it was pointless?'

'The interesting question is why you think this journey will address your sense of absence.'

'I don't know. I suppose Richard Wardner has come to represent something to me.'

'A symbol perhaps? A symbol of what is missing from your life?'

'Yes,' Sam said, leaning towards him. 'Yes, that's it.'

'Yet I am sure you know, a symbol is just that. It only means what you want it to.'

'That's true.'

'I do wonder if the modern world,' he said, straightening his collar, 'creates these desperations for you. It makes you crave products you don't want. It places its imperatives in front of religion, faith. It employs certain people for its cause. Celebrities, singers, musicians. When you conclude that the material world is disappointing you look to these figures for answers, as they sit just beyond the array. You hunt these figures down, like they are wise men. If they vanish from your life you imbue them as symbols with even greater potency. But really it is what you project onto them that's interesting.'

The prior weaved his fingers together, as toast popped up behind him. 'Jam, butter?'

Sam shrugged.

He moved back into the kitchen. 'You feel that if you find this Wardner, then with him you find the answer?'

'That might be it.'

'So, if you found him would you feel as if you had come to the end of your journey?'

There was a hint of mischief playing around the prior's lips as he returned, with a pile of toast, jam jars balancing on top of it.

'No,' Sam said.

The prior waved a finger at Sam. 'No you wouldn't. Because your quest is spiritual. You seek to fill the void, don't you?'

'That void will always exist though.' Sam spooned jam onto a slice, and took a bite. 'Until I succeed at something.'

'I see.' He looked through the window. 'Now, I must show you the grounds. Here, bring your coffee.'

The sunlight was just starting to break over the hills behind them, lighting up the rectangular allotment on which men bustled. Sam sipped the cooling coffee as he followed the prior. 'With a spiritual retreat comes the opportunity to learn new skills,' he said. 'To put something back into the earth.'

Sam eyed the rows of marrows and radishes.

'You can take these straight out of the ground and into the pan?'

'There is only one way to address your scepticism.'

'I'm not sure I can carry a bunch of marrows on the train,' Sam said.

The prior laughed.

'See what you think of this.'

They moved over to the small patch of turf near the back gate, where a man was bent double, concerning himself with something laid on the soil.

'There's nothing here,' Sam said.

'Not yet, but there will be soon, won't there?'

The prior wasn't addressing Sam, but the man at his feet. As Sam moved to ask him what he was growing he found himself looking straight into the face of Robert Wardner.

The singer was visibly aged, the faint lines that Sam had seen in so many photographs now deep crevices. Despite his position in the bright sunlight Wardner looked ravaged, a sinewy man in a camouflage jacket, his hair hacked short. His shaking fingers quivering through the dirt. He was indistinguishable from it, a whisper through the looming pines. He was part of something invigorating, and yet he looked as if he was barely of this realm.

The prior stooped to address him.

'I'm afraid our visitor isn't convinced about what we are trying to do out here.'

Wardner looked slowly up at Sam.

'Perhaps we should tell our visitor,' Wardner said, 'that these days people don't understand work.'

His voice was gruffer than Sam had expected, barely recognisable from the songs and interviews.

The prior stepped back, placed his hands on his hips. 'Be my guest,' he said.

Sam decided to speak first. 'I'm not saying it won't grow. I'm just thinking it's a lot of effort for a few vegetables. Isn't it?'

Wardner's eyes passed over Sam, with a chemical blankness that Sam had never seen before. Slowly, he opened his mouth.

'Where you come from, my friend, people only work at things if they can leave their mark on it. They don't care about vegetables, because they don't come with a credit. But down here,' his trembling hands pointed into the earth, 'work is about making something that sustains. That doesn't have a stamp.'

The prior nodded.

Sam's eyes traced over Wardner's tattoos, unable to believe who he was talking to. Yet the evidence was all there. That line from Hamlet, still in faint black ink on his left arm.

The prior could pull me away at any moment, Sam thought. I've got to seize this chance.

'But what about art?' Sam said. 'Art can help others, and move your career forward too can't it?'

Wardner's lips began to move again, with a curl of bitterness edging into them. 'So you know who I am.'

'I think you can help him, Robert,' the prior said.

Wardner nodded deferentially, his glazed eyes slowly moving back to Sam.

'Art will collapse, son, because the internet screwed your generation over. Everyone can have a go at making something and putting it on the web.'

Wardner stood up, and straightened. 'But it's not art,' he continued. 'It's just noise, made by people trying to shout loudest. There'll be so much of it one day it'll all collapse.'

His hands moved, slender as autumn leaves, as he spoke. Sam could only equate the feeling it provoked with the one he experienced walking along the beach, when it all got too much in his youth.

'So all that work will be lost?'

Wardner looked to the hills, as if addressing the sprawl that lay beyond it. 'Someone will own it. But it won't be you.'

Sam felt the wind around him, the heat of it energising him. He pulled his coat tighter around himself. 'So you're saying I shouldn't believe in art?'

'If you've got no loved ones, it's not a bad place to look for answers. Artists are better visionaries than celebrities, who they're often confused with. But if you can find people who care about you, don't neglect them for art. Look to sustaining others, rather than yourself.'

'No one ever advises us to do that.'

'Culture always tells you to look to illusions for answers. 'Look at me', it says, 'I've worked it all out'. Celebrities grow too powerful because people mistake their colour for content. They allow them to create a hole at the heart of our culture, in which they then flourish.'

'Is that why you're out here then? You've had enough of that culture?'

There seemed a change in the wind.

'I have to be here. Unlike you, I don't have a choice.'

Wardner's eyes, flecked with grey, flickered.

'I'm a journalist who wrote about your music, Mr Wardner. I know that the rumours about you killing that young fan aren't true. Nataly told me what is true.'

Wardner widened his eyes. At that moment, a small sparrow alighted on the fence behind him. Wardner watched it preen itself.

'Nataly,' he said. 'So Nataly gave me away.'

'I don't think she gave you away. I think she's perhaps offered you your freedom, to be honest. You see, she told me that Bonny created that rumour. But I know there's nothing in it. The police aren't after you, and you can return home. I know why she told me you had killed a man too. To scare me off finding you.'

Wardner stood up straight, the effort seemingly paining him. 'No,' he said. 'That's not true. Nataly would never play games like that. The truth is, I did kill a man.'

'Robert?' The prior's voice had dropped to a whisper, as he placed his hand on Wardner's shoulder.

'It was an accident,' he answered. 'His name was Andrew Cunningham, and he was the head of our record label. We were having a bitter fight about our album. I had been devoted to recording it for years. Cunningham wanted to rush it out before we were ready. I was a younger man then, prior, with a short fuse. We both said a few vicious things, and our manager had to hold me back. I threatened...' He stopped, and coughed for a moment.

'It's alright,' the prior said.

'I threatened to strangle him. It was only once Bonny had calmed me down that I saw him, collapsed on the floor. The heart attack killed him instantly.'

'That's not murder,' the prior said.

'He's right,' echoed Sam. 'And I have seen the coroner's report. It didn't implicate you in any way.'

Wardner coughed. A hacking, unhinged cough that built until

it threatened to send him into spasms.

The prior lowered his voice, drawing Sam away. 'Let's discuss this another time. It isn't fair to put all this on Robert.'

Wardner shook his head. 'I knew that Cunningham had a weak heart. At various points I encouraged Simon, my guitarist, to give him ecstasy. I joked that it would send his ticker into overdrive. I didn't want him to die, much as I hated him. I was just showing off. But I know it is only a matter of time until someone asks Simon about it under oath and I'll be done for. Subconsciously, I think I provoked Cunningham knowing that it would kill him.'

'That's still not murder,' Sam said.

'That's enough,' the prior said. 'We should leave Robert alone now.'

Sam felt guilty at having taken so much out of the singer with his questions. It was as if each of Wardner's expressions had cost Wardner another chunk of his flesh. Until now he was a husk, assimilated by wind and earth, which crept from the hills and seeped through the soil, pulling him prematurely into their fortified cycles. Sam and the prior drew away.

'When he arrived here,' the prior said, 'he was close to death. We are in the early stages of trying to claw him back. We give him only light duties.'

He placed a hand on Sam's shoulder. 'Sam, just as I have respected your journey in bringing it to a close, you must also respect his and not give away his place of rest.'

Sam nodded slowly. 'I just can't believe it.'

'Your train,' the prior said. 'You will miss your train.'

Sam pressed a palm to his head. 'I don't know how I can thank you. Even if I can't use this, it means the world to me...'

'Thank me by honouring what I asked of you. I am putting my faith in you.'

19

Camille eased into her chair on the terrace, the straps of her black summer dress falling around her shoulders. She peered through the hanging baskets, down to the bustling city below. As Sam opened the door to come onto the terrace the sound of a piano from inside filtered out to Camille. As he moved into her vision she pulled off her sunglasses and smiled up at him.

Around them young couples whispered, paused to sip cocktails and drew from cigarettes. They then tilted their heads back, blowing jets of smoke up at the shimmering blue sky.

He moved to greet her. Sam noticed that her bare shoulders had begun to tan, ringlets from her pinned-up hair playing on her neck as he sat opposite.

'It's so good to see you,' she said, her lips pursing around a straw.

A tightness seemed to have gone from underneath her eyes. He imagined her in a basement room in Paris, singing along to an old vinyl as rain teased the window. In her own private world.

'How are you?'

'I'm good, Sam. In fact, I have some news.'

'I'm listening.'

'I've left Mason House.'

'Really? Why?'

'Sam! Because of your book!'

'I didn't cause you to lose your job?'

'No, you didn't 'cause me to lose my job'. You caused me to get offered a new one!'

Sam waved over a waiter, and ordered a San Miguel. Camille kept smiling. The buttery scent from her exposed skin enticed him.

'I don't understand,' he said.

'Martin canned the book, Sam. He thought it was damaging

his reputation. There's nothing he cares about more, except perhaps the welfare of Siberian snow leopards.'

'I guessed that already. He gave me a day to find Wardner, and we've not spoken since.'

'Sam, I'm sorry.' She reached for her sunglasses but decided to leave them. 'The controversy was too much for him. But there's more.' She placed her hand on his arm . 'I've been offered a job at Harder and Wells. A bigger publisher, where I have much more influence. Working for someone who actually appreciates my rare gift for...'

'Appreciating overlooked bands from the eighties?'

'Exactly.'

'So how does this affect me?'

'Very greatly, Sam. Because my first order of business is to take on your new book.'

'No.'

'And pay you the advance you are well overdue.'

Behind him a couple laughed. He wanted to join them, toast the news. The sky seemed to bloom with exuberance. The waiter returned, Camille leaning in to ensure she didn't miss any of Sam's reaction as his beer was placed. Sam smiled, looking down at the golden bubbles. Watching them mingle and dance. She seemed to be following his reaction so carefully.

'It's as simple as that? I can't believe it.'

'It's never completely simple, Sam.'

'Go on.'

'They don't want a straight quest book, like a journalist would tell. They want something more creative.'

'Which would require an interview with Wardner?'

'No,' she laughed. 'Don't worry about that. They have agreed to commission a book about your journey to track him down, regardless of if you found him. The controversy you've courted is enough to guarantee book sales. But to put a fresh twist on the biography format they suggested having part of it written as if from Wardner's perspective.'

'What, like his journal?'

'Will that be too difficult?'

'Well, there was something I never told Elsa during our whole relationship. I knew it was weird, and I thought it would freak her out.'

'What?'

'When I was younger....when I was a bit too obsessed... I tried to do just that. Write Wardner's account of his own disappearance. An autobiography in his absence.'

'Shut up.'

'It's true.'

She sipped. 'You could finish it then. I'm sure that we can find a way to make it work. Isn't it great news?'

He took it all in. The sound of the piano keys through the open door, the seductive margin of sun around rustling plants.

'I can't believe you quit over my book.'

'I'd have been fired soon anyway. Martin's been threatening to employ only vegans for ages. And the book wasn't his idea.'

'What do you mean?'

'I found out when I quit that it was Theo who got in touch with Mason House. Suggested getting someone to track down Wardner. Perhaps it was he who leaked your address to the fans?'

'No wonder he wouldn't tell me where Wardner was. He wanted me to show him.'

'I think Theo was hoping to drum up some excitement about the band. Push Wardner to reform it, given all the speculation that would create.'

'I wonder if Bonny was in cahoots with him. It looked that way at his gig. I think perhaps she wanted to get me even more immersed in the mythology around Robert. She wouldn't have minded me raising her profile and helping her sell her art, either.'

'Would she go to such effort just to do that?'

'You didn't get to talk to her like I did. It was pretty clear that she felt Robert took her career off her. Made her start afresh. I think, one way or another, she was pretty keen to finally make good on her investment in him.'

Sam tilted his head back. 'So the fans know Theo was responsible for the effort to find Wardner. Not me?'

'They do now. So they'll blame Theo for pushing him back into hiding, not you.'

'That could explain why whoever was threatening me has stopped. I think it was Wardner's cousin. I can see how he might have got hold of my address now, too.'

'Did the police take any finger prints?'

'Yes, but since the grief has stopped I haven't followed it up.'

'He must have been genuinely scared that you'd find Robert.'

Sam took a deep draught.

'Camille, I have something to tell you.'

'What?'

'I've been wondering during this whole conversation if I should tell you. But I did find Wardner.'

She dropped the straw, and grasped his hand. It was slender, and cool, and Sam had to focus on not reacting to it.

'What?'

He nodded. 'I'm telling you, I met Wardner. Living in seclusion, somewhere in the hills. But I was sworn to secrecy about exactly where…'

'Oh my God.'

'And I'm not going to break that promise.'

'You met Wardner? My goodness. What was he like? What happened?'

Sam held the beer, and in a reckless moment decided to act on impulse.

'How about we discuss it over dinner?'

Camille leant back and laughed. Looked over the teeming city. Then back at Sam.

'Only way you'll find out, Camille.'

'Okay, you've twisted my arm, Sam. But bear in mind, any man could have offered that and I'd have said yes.'

'I'll take what I'm given.'

Her eyes widened with disbelief.

'You sure you don't want to use it for the book?'

'Definitely not.'

'There are so many ways round it though,' she said, flapping her hands in excitement. 'You could change the names and destinations. Obscure the details. Persuade a ghost-writer to tell your story as if it is fiction.'

'Yes, boss.'

She laughed.

Sam followed the sound of it as it faded, into the warmth that emanated from the terrace. This evening now seemed greater than the sum of its parts, an expansive atmosphere that was open for Sam to explore. He closed his eyes. Thought of Elsa, of the threats, of the deserted house and the draining silences. All behind him. All part of a story he could now contain on the page.

When he looked up Camille was smiling to herself.

'Right,' he said. 'The band will be about to start.'

He was glad the band didn't embarrass him, having persuaded Camille to cross the road to the Star And Garter. It was a young group who wore shirts spray-painted with slogans like 'Destroy Culture' and 'Disconnect Yourself'. They threw themselves recklessly around the tiny stage, expressing themselves through a barrage of sound. Although Sam didn't know their songs he knew their shapes, their anger, well in advance.

During their final song Camille decided to dance and she pulled Sam to the front of the packed basement. They were almost close enough to the band to be hit by flailing fret boards. The younger punters greeted his enthusiasm with a smile, and for once Sam didn't feel self-conscious. Every time the main riff of the song came around Camille piled her now loosened thick, dark hair on top of her head and let it fall in time to the song. The act transfixed Sam. She seemed to know it.

After the band had left a DJ began to play some records and everyone rushed onto the makeshift dance floor. It was Sam who pulled Camille onto it, when the catchy opening to 'Commuter Belt' prised everyone from tattered seats and into the throng.

The room danced, with their hands above their head. 'We're all part of the same cult now', they sang. A strange chorus line of dark leather, hairspray and nail varnish.

These people are made of the same awkward substance as me, Sam thought. People like us never quite adjust to the world, only fully understand it through the records we live through.

Even though The National Grid wouldn't reform Sam realized then how their music endured. In under-attended discos, late night parties and, perhaps most importantly, in private reflections. Sam suspected he would soon turn to their music again, to help him take on a world that had finally begun to open.

Acknowledgements

Thanks to Lynette Rasco for the cover photo. This book was written and researched over the course of three years as part of a Creative Writing PhD at Northumbria University. I am grateful to have had the time afforded by a studentship, for a year and a half, to work on it. I am hugely indebted to my PhD supervisors for their kind and enduring support. During the course of researching this book I was fortunate to interview various post-punk artists. Thank you especially to Jehnny Beth and Julie Campbell. Thank you also to Hanna and Lyn for your support, and to Norah Perkins at Curtis Brown. I was fortunate to benefit from the insight of such a great range of authors, editors, musicians and agents. This book is dedicated to my wife, Bethany.

At Roundfire we publish great stories. We lean towards the spiritual and thought-provoking. But whether it's literary or popular, a gentle tale or a pulsating thriller, the connecting theme in all Roundfire fiction titles is that once you pick them up you won't want to put them down.